CHAOS RISING

AUTHOR:

James Collura

EDITOR:

Jeff Harkness

ART DIRECTOR:

Casey Christofferson

LAYOUT:

Suzy Moseby

5E CONVERSION:

Scott McKinley with Edwin Nagy

INTERIOR ART:

Santa Norvaisaite, Adrian Landeros, Brett Barkley

FRONT COVER ART:

Michael Syrigos

CARTOGRAPHY:

Robert Altbauer

COVER DESIGN:

Casey Christofferson

PLAYTESTERS:

Brain Mursch, Alex Yang, Courtney Brownlee, Adam Freeman, Adam Moran, Lionel Thompson, Scott Turnbull, Jorge Santiago, and Serge Clermont.

SPECIAL THANKS:

To Brenda, the love of my life, for encouraging me to write this module; to Brian & Alex for all of their support; to Clark & Bill for the opportunity to be part of a great team; to Casey & Lance for all of their assistance; and to my parents for fostering my love for reading and for buying me a red box, a white crayon, six blue dice, and a book that unlocked my imagination.

NECROMANCER Games™

FROG GOD GAMES

ISBN: 978-1-62283-942-1

5e Softcover

TABLE OF CONTENTS

CHAOS RISING

By James Collura

An adventure for 4 to 6 Tier 3 characters.

INTRODUCTION

A challenging adventure for four to six Tier 3 characters, **Chaos Rising** offers an excellent add-on to any fantasy campaign. The location of the Devil's Finger — the main site of the adventure — can be placed in any mountain chain. The benefactor the characters serve is generic and customizable for your campaign; where the party meets the benefactor is similarly up to your discretion. The deities presented in the adventure — Dwurfater, Orcus, and the Faceless Lord — may also be changed to fit your campaign. The major enemy, Lord Raob, could easily be a reoccurring enemy in the campaign. The timing of the adventure is a fortnight before a blood moon. Since blood moons are rare and not easily predictable, this event could be added to your campaign at any time.

The adventure begins when a benefactor implores the characters to take on a nearly impossible quest to retrieve a demon's amulet. First, the heroes must scale a 750-foot-tall monument to reach an ancient dwarven castle known in modern times as the Citadel. Arriving at the Citadel, the characters evade the machinations of an evil lord and travel through time to acquire a key that unlocks an ancient vault created by a long-forgotten demon prince. In the Citadel, the heroes confront both demons and undead. Once the key is obtained, the characters wait for the appointed hour: the rising of a blood moon. Once the vault is bathed in the rising moon's crimson glow, the adventure concludes as the characters enter the vault, awaken and confront the avatar of a demon prince, and recover pieces of a riddle that allows them to seize the prince's amulet.

THE LEGEND OF THE FACELESS LORD

In the beginning, when the fires of creation cooled and the first mortals began to walk the Material Plane, the greater gods gathered to divide the multiverse. Those of weal took the most pleasant planes. They shared these planes with their allies and made them as they saw fit. Thus, the heavens were created. As well, some of the evil spawned by creation banded together and formed a great army that seized the remaining planes. Thus, the hells were created. These lords of hell demanded tribute from all of evil bent. Along with this tribute, they demanded subservience to their will and rule.

Not all were happy with this division between good and evil. Some were left with only the most inhospitable and deformed areas of the multiverse. These beings challenged this so-called natural order of the celestials and the devils. They cried out in dissension and formed a great horde that ravaged the planes. These were the first demons. Sent forth to lead an army of celestials against the demons was a being of absolute rigidity and perfection. His body was fair and his mind keen. This beacon of light had no visage but a perfectly smooth face from which blinding light emitted. He was known as the Faceless Lord.

Unfortunately, the Faceless Lord was led astray during the battles with the demons. He learned to revel in his brilliance on the battlefield, and so his vanity was his undoing. He began to see the demons not as the vile beacons of lawlessness, but as oppressed beings subjugated by both celestials and devils. Soon, he was swayed to the side of disorder and led many of his celestial followers to the dark. Who tempted this icon of perfection? Orcus? Demogorgon? Who can say?

What is known is that when the combined armies of the good-aligned planes overtook the demonic hordes, they cast the demons into the Abyss, the worst of all planes. To mark his sin permanently, the greater gods of good stripped the Faceless Lord of his perfection. He became a liquefied and ever-changing deity. Some say that a certain greater power remarked that this was done so all would know the Faceless Lord for what he was: ever-changing and devoid of trust. The Faceless Lord is the personification of chaos. He is always changing, always plotting, and always thoroughly evil. He is known by some as Jubilex.

ADVENTURE BACKGROUND

The adventure begins at the Devil's Finger, a 750-foot-tall granite monument. At the apex of this monolith is an ancient and abandoned dwarven castle. Although the true name of the castle is Dwurschmiede, this name is lost to the ages, and the castle is known in modern times simply as the Citadel. The Citadel surrounds a gigantic cube of obsidian. Impervious to magic, the true nature of the Obsidian Vault is known to only a few scholars.

The Obsidian Vault is a creation of Jubilex, the Faceless Lord. Like most powerful demons, the Faceless Lord spent considerable effort in hiding his soul, which was made manifest in the form of an amulet. To protect his amulet, the Faceless Lord created the Obsidian Vault. Crafted from the then-dwindling fires of creation, the Obsidian Vault is impervious to everything, whether magical or mundane, mortal or divine. After placing his soul within the vault, the Faceless Lord let loose the great cube and sent it wandering through the planes.

For reasons unknown, several thousand years ago, the vault appeared on the characters' home plane and crashed on top of a mountain. As a result of the magical energies that protect the vault, combined with the force of the impact, the Devil's Finger was formed. Ancient dwarves discovered and revered the monolith as a work of wonder. Soon, some wicked dwarves began to revere the Faceless Lord on the grounds that, out of chaos, he constructed the vault, an example of nearly perfect craftsmanship. Since the dwarven pantheon abhors chaos, the leader of the dwarven gods, Dwurfater, grew wrathful.

The vault's protections were beyond even the power of Dwurfater to breach. Using all of his strength, Dwurfater could not penetrate the vault. Only through placating the inherent evilness of the vault by sacrificing dwarven lives did Dwurfater gather the strength to bore an opening through the stone and create a door. As tears ran down Dwurfater's face, many dwarves gave their lives to aid their god in his task. Blood washed the entire Devil's Finger as generations of dwarves were sacrificed for this gruesome but necessary deed.

Though the penetration was finally accomplished, Dwurfater was too weakened to open the door he created and seize control of the amulet, so with his last bit of strength he crafted a key such that mortals could accomplish what he could not. The Faceless Lord learned of what Dwurfater planned and attempted to stop the followers from securing the amulet that contained his soul. Arriving at the Citadel, the Faceless Lord's avatar rushed after Dwurfater's disciples and entered the vault.

In the battle that ensued between the Faceless Lord and Dwurfater's followers, the dwarves accomplished their true task: As the Faceless Lord entered the vault, Dwurfater's strength returned, and he closed the door. The Faceless Lord was trapped inside with his amulet.

After this great victory by the dwarves, they built Dwurschmiede, the Citadel, a structure designed to safeguard the vault. The Citadel was to bar those who would seek to free the Faceless Lord or take his amulet for themselves. Also, the Citadel was created to guard the key used by Dwurfater to lock the vault. To remember the bloody sacrifice of the dwarves and to placate the evil that imprisons the Faceless Lord, the door to the vault appears only once every 400 years when a blood moon rises and bathes the Devil's Finger in an unnatural red light.

Dwurfater assisted in the creation of the Citadel. He infused his divinity into the Citadel to protect the only means of returning the Faceless Lord to the world: the key. One protection prevents anyone from directly accessing any other plane (such as the Astral Plane for teleportation) while on the Devil's Finger. This divine infusion also prevents anyone from contacting an evil-aligned plane for divination, summoning, or other purposes.

The second protection is stronger and unusually arcane for the dwarves. To the outside world, the Citadel appears as a great fortress with towers and walls encircling the vault. This appearance is merely a ruse, however. Through Dwurfater's guidance and divinity, these outer walls and defenses are a façade protecting the Citadel's true nature: its interior is actually a demiplane.

The interior of the Citadel exists and ages the same as the outer world. Entrance to the Citadel, however, is limited to a single planar gate inside a great barbican. This planar gate is far from simple, for it uses temporal wells to send intruders through time. Only with a *portal rune* (described in **Chapter One** and **Appendix A**) can someone gain access to the actual Citadel.

Within this interior demiplane, an entire clan of dwarves — Clan Flammeaxte — willingly submitted to living apart as protectors of the Citadel. Their mission was simple: prevent anyone from acquiring the key.

To further guard the key, Dwurfater fashioned a second demiplane. Like the first planar gate, the second gate uses time itself as a defense. Only with a special rune known only to the lord or king of the Citadel may one enter this second plane. In the second plane, the dwarves created many wards and guardians to protect the key. Disguising the second demiplane as catacombs to baffle aggressors, the dwarves have thus far succeeded in their task. No one has acquired the key.

During the millennia since the first dwarves stood guard in the Citadel, many armies have marched on the Devil's Finger seeking the key as a first step to acquiring the demon's amulet. Even with the temporal portals, the clan of dwarves, and the confusion created by shifts in time and space, evil was undeterred from acquiring the Faceless Lord's amulet-soul.

Two such undeterred armies were those of the demon prince Orcus and, later, a legion of undead commanded by a powerful priest named Giltz. Orcus, a deceiver, learned of the Citadel's nature. Knowing that Dwurfater's protections prevented

direct entry, Orcus turned a goodly priest to evil and taught him a way to overcome the protection and open a *gate* to Orcus' home plane. Eventually, possibly with the characters' help, the dwarves pushed back the demons and closed the unusual gate.

Later, Giltz accomplished what Orcus could not: He and a host of undead overcame and wiped out the dwarves. Yet before Giltz could claim his prize, the last dwarves assassinated him. In his anguish, Giltz's spirit remained and now haunts the Citadel's demiplane.

Currently, the Citadel abides in a parallel plane but is abandoned and its purpose lost to the minds of human and dwarf alike. So, too, is the name of the Faceless Lord forgotten. Knowledge of him is only a whisper among those who study the arcane. To this day, the Faceless Lord stirs trapped within the vault, nursing a hatred of all dwarves. For the ironic secret of the vault, the Faceless Lord created is this: though the vault is a reliquary for the Faceless Lord's amulet, it also serves as his prison.

This situation is about to change, however. The evil Lord Raob Blackenheart has gathered an army and encamped it at the summit of the Devil's Finger. Here, he and his men are excavating the Citadel and attempting to dig down to the key's resting place. This strategy is folly, for Raob has yet to suspect that the now-ruined towers and walls are merely a ruse. It is only a matter of time before this evil lord learns of the Citadel's true nature and acquires the key.

A blood moon approaches in two weeks' time.

Enter the characters. Through the hook of your choosing, they are charged with a daunting task: acquire the key, spoil an evil lord's machinations, open the vault, and save the world — all in a day's work for heroes.

ADVENTURE HOOKS

The adventure begins when the characters learn portions of the background from a benefactor such as a church (good or evil) or a guild (wizards or thieves), as fits your campaign and particular characters. Whichever organization or individual ultimately employs the characters, that entity is referred to hereafter as the benefactor. The benefactor's primary motivation is to obtain a demon price's amulet. What the benefactor wishes to do with the amulet depends on several issues. For example, a goodly church would wish to destroy the device, while a wizards' guild would want to study it, and an evil sect would want to use its powers to further their own fell agenda.

Here are several suggested hooks:

- One of the characters owes a great debt to the benefactor, and the benefactor is now asking that the debt be paid. In a good-aligned campaign, now is the time to pay up for all that free healing at the local church. In an evil-aligned campaign, the benefactor could attempt to assassinate one of the characters and blame Raob. During that time, the benefactor approaches the characters with the helpful information as to who is trying to kill them. The benefactor lets them know of Raob.

- An agent of the Faceless Lord could hire the characters. The characters have no idea that their benefactor works for the fallen celestial. Still, the characters rush off to save the day not knowing that their actions loose the Faceless Lord on the world. This is a difficult scenario because of the horrific twist that will likely take place assuming the characters overcome the Faceless Lord, just to learn seconds after their victory that they were the pawns of chaos.

- If you do not want to use a benefactor, you could have the party's wizard or other spellcaster learn of the Citadel while deep into studying a recently acquired tome (conveniently placed in the prior adventure). In the margins of the tome are notes by Sleeara, the necromancer serving Raob. The party's researcher puts together what Sleeara is planning, the location of the Citadel, and the time remaining to stop her.

Basically, **Chaos Rising** can take place at any time and in virtually any locale. You should be creative in starting the adventure and impress upon the characters the grave danger that threatens the realm if Raob takes the amulet for himself.

The characters and the benefactor should know a few key facts (or acquire such information from the tome, if using that hook), including the existence of the Citadel, the existence of the key, and that a demon prince's amulet lies within the vault. The benefactor should also know that Lord Raob is attempting to seize the amulet for himself. Furthermore, through an astrologer, the benefactor knows that a blood moon approaches in 14 days.

Finally, the benefactor has discovered that there is a portal into the Citadel. The benefactor might believe, as Raob does, that the Citadel is in ruins and therefore, the passageways and tunnels that lead to the key are collapsed and full of rubble. Therefore, to beat Raob to the key, the characters must use the portal, travel back through time to where the passageways are intact, and snatch the key out from under Raob.

To activate the portal, the benefactor has employed an ancient dwarven priestess. This priestess actually knows the Citadel's planar secret, but does not disclose this information under any circumstances. Instead, she marks or tattoos the necessary *portal rune* (see **Appendix A**) on all the characters' necks to allow them access in an effort to destroy the Faceless Lord once and for all.

The important fact that is omitted in any setup for this adventure (although wily characters might correctly guess this fact) is that the Faceless Lord is trapped within the vault. Thus, the characters should be unaware of this matter at the time they embark upon their quest.

Players' Introduction

With a minimum of alteration, the following background is usable for most any benefactor or hook you choose — good or evil, arcane, divine, or worldly. Read or paraphrase as necessary:

The heavy eyes of your benefactor peer over the tomes and scrolls on her desk to look you square in the eye. She awaits an answer.

You and your friends received the summons less than a week ago. The urgency in tone could not be mistaken — grave danger threatens the realm.

You have been asked to retrieve a fabulous artifact, the amulet of a demon prince. Like most who have studied or encountered demons before, you know that a demon's amulet contains its soul. One who possesses such an artifact can banish the demon for centuries or even command it to heed one's will. Thus, the amulet of a minor demon in the wrong hands can be a force of destruction. The amulet of a demon prince can render anyone invincible.

To accomplish this quest, you must travel to an arid mountain chain. In the midst of these mountains stands a gigantic granite monument 750 feet high that resembles the bony knuckles of a finger. It is known as the Devil's Finger. On top of the Devil's Finger lies an ancient fortress carved directly out of the granite. Legends tell that the fortress, known today simply as the Citadel, was built by ancient dwarves. The entire complex has collapsed and is in ruins.

The dwarves built the Citadel around a gigantic cube — or vault — of obsidian. The origin of the vault is unknown; however, religious scholars working for your benefactor think that it is otherworldly in nature and predates the Citadel. Thus, these scholars assume that the Citadel was built to protect the vault.

Within the vault, the amulet lies undisturbed as it has for thousands of years. Armies laid siege to the Citadel hoping to acquire the key and the amulet. Breaking their attacks against the granite, no army succeeded. Now that no one guards the key, however, the evil Lord Raob Blackenheart might succeed where others have failed.

Although few texts and histories concerning the Citadel are extant, what is known is that once every 400 years a blood moon rises and reveals an entrance to the vault. If someone stands at the entrance at this appointed hour with a special key, then he may enter the vault. No other means magical or otherwise can penetrate the cube. The key is presumed to reside in a complex of caves and catacombs beneath the Citadel.

Your benefactor had very little interest in the Citadel until a month ago, when after 1,200 years it once again became occupied. Apparently, the evil Lord Raob and his pet necromancer are determined to find the key and open the cube. They and a small army are camped around the ruins of the Citadel and are attempting to dig their way through the collapsed halls and find the key. Going by his reputation for malice and slaughter, Raob likely intends to take the amulet and begin a campaign of carnage and bloodshed.

Your benefactor has employed astrologers and learned that a blood moon approaches in a fortnight. Your party is asked to climb the Devil's Finger, enter the Citadel, and steal the key before Lord Raob succeeds.

Naturally, this task will not be easy. First, numerous magical protections are still active in the Devil's Finger. These protections make scaling the monument with extreme caution necessary. In addition, the presence of Lord Raob and his army requires you to use stealth. Once you are on top of the Devil's Finger, you must find the main entrance to the Citadel. This entrance is believed to be within a massive barbican.

Your benefactor has devised an unusual way for you to acquire the key before Lord Raob. One of the protections that the dwarves used involved magical portals that allowed guards to travel back through time to warn of invaders. Your benefactor's scholars presume that two such portals remain today. One is at the entrance to the entrance to the Citadel's top level, and the other is a hidden entrance into the catacombs where the key lies.

Thus, you will use these portals to shift to a time when the passageways are not blocked by rock and rubble. In this alternate reality or time, the Citadel is in its full splendor, and you should therefore be able to acquire the key and return to your home time. Your benefactor has convinced an ancient dwarven priestess to inscribe the necessary *portal rune* on each of you. This tattoo will be placed on your neck and under no circumstance should fall into enemy's hands. Although nothing is known of the denizens of this other time, they should prove less hostile than dealing with Lord Raob and his army.

Once the key is acquired, your task is not over. Retrieving the key and foiling the evil lord's plans is not enough. This evil must be ended once and for all so that future generations are not caught unaware. You must enter the cube on the night of the blood moon, retrieve this amulet, and return it so that it may be destroyed, ending the vileness of the demon prince's essence.

Your benefactor's stare breaks for a moment. She licks her cracked lips and speaks harshly, "What say thee?"

Running the Adventure

The characters start by meeting with their benefactor. After this meeting, the characters have an opportunity to prepare for the assault on the Devil's Finger, purchase supplies and items, and plan for the adventure. The benefactor also provides the characters with a device or key to activate the portals.

As explained in the Adventure Background, the characters have a fortnight to scale the Devil's Finger and retrieve an item known simply as the key. The key allows the characters to enter the vault (during a blood moon) and attempt to take the demon's amulet. The challenge is presented in five stages.

Stage One: Assaulting the Devil's Finger (The Present)

Described in **Chapter One**, the characters must find their way into the Citadel. The Devil's Finger stands more than 750 feet tall. The challenge lies in arriving at the top of the monument without alerting Lord Raob. One obvious option is to climb the cliff face; however, not only are guards patrolling the perimeter, but several gargoyles act as natural guardians. The characters will more likely use magical means to arrive atop the great pillar. Some magical energies, such as teleportation, are suppressed by enchantments still active in the Citadel. So, arriving on top of the Devil's Finger without Raob noticing will not be easy for the characters. In addition, using magic might prove more dangerous than climbing because of a series of magical alarms that alert the small army commanded by Lord Raob and Sleeara. A third option is to use the makeshift elevator that Lord Raob uses. This approach should also prove difficult, owing to the army guards that protect the elevator. Although these guards might be easily overcome, they could sound an alarm that brings an entire army down on the characters. Once on top of the Devil's Finger, the characters penetrate the barbican near where Raob's archaeological operation is underway. After arriving, the party passes through the portal, which is activated by their personal *portal rune* (see **Appendix A**), in an effort presumably to bypass hundreds of feet of rock and rubble.

Stage Two: Entering the Portal and the Siege of Orcus (3,000 Years in the Past)

As described in **Chapter Three**, the second stage of the adventure begins once the party passes through the portal, which allows the party to enter the Citadel's demiplane. Whether the characters perceive of the change in planes is ultimately up to you. The interior of the Citadel has two portals that allow such travel through time or space. The first portal is the entrance to the Citadel's Upper Halls, the second is an archway in the Lower Halls that leads to the catacombs where the key lies.

The upper archway sends the characters to "The Siege of Orcus," an alternate plane that is similar in every way to the characters' home plane, save that the Siege of Orcus occurs almost 3,000 years in the past. Remember that the Citadel's demiplane and the characters' home plane move through time — or, age — at the same rate, but due to the planar gate's temporal nature, the characters have gone back through time. The Citadel is simply inaccessible except through the barbican portal.

During the "Siege of Orcus," the characters appear at the start of a siege by the forces of the demon prince Orcus, who desires the Faceless Lord's amulet for himself. Specifically, the characters appear shortly before Orcus bypasses the magical wards of the Citadel and opens a *gate*. Using this gate, a group of demons attempts to seize the dwarven king who holds the rune to access the catacombs. The characters may or may not assist them in defending the Citadel, although success might be impossible without assisting them. The characters' prime goal is to find the lower portal that will send them to the catacombs demiplane where the key lies.

Stage Three: Acquiring the Key (The Present)

Leaving the "siege of Orcus" behind, the characters enter the catacombs as explained in **Chapter Four**. Again, the characters change planes and travel through time — to the present. Like the Citadel, this demiplane moves through time at the same rate as the party's home plane; however, the portal's temporal nature sends the characters to another era.

The catacombs were built for the dwarven kings who served the Citadel. The use of the crypts is to hide the real purpose of the area: to protect and guard the key. At the very bottom of this area is the complex with the key. The acquisition of the key is the characters' primary goal.

Stage Four: The Return Journey and Necromantic Dreams (1,200 Years in the Past)

In **Chapter Four**, after acquiring the key, the characters return through the lower archway and travel back to the Citadel's demiplane. The characters do not, though, return to the time of the Siege of Orcus. Instead, they are sent to "Necromantic Dreams," where an army of undead decimated the dwarves. These events take place on the Citadel's demiplane 1,200 years in the past from the time of the characters' home plane. Approximately 100 years before the characters' arrival, the powerful priest led an army in an effort to take the amulet. The priest died during the final assault, so the undead have settled in the Citadel.

The "Siege of Orcus" is described in **Chapter Three**, and "Necromantic Dreams" is described in **Chapter Five**. The different rooms and physical features of the Citadel itself are detailed in **Chapter Two**, which also details various NPC parties that are seeking the key. In other words, the characters will traverse the same dungeon at least twice, but with different sets of encounters for each sojourn.

Stage Five: Confronting the Faceless Lord (The Present)

Once the characters leave the Citadel and return to their home plane and time with the key, they may have to deal with Lord Raob and wait for the blood moon that appears at the end of the fortnight. Raob and Sleeara are possibly one of the groups of time-traveling NPCs that the characters confront during the "Siege of Orcus" or "Necromantic Dreams." During the interim between acquiring the key and the blood moon's rising, the characters may vanquish Lord Raob or perhaps join forces with him, if they are so inclined. Raob may also quite possibly discover that the Citadel was a façade and out of frustration decide to take his army elsewhere. In any event, once the blood moon rises, the characters should use the key and enter the vault of the demon prince. These events are explained in **Chapter Six**.

Within the strange obsidian cube, the characters find themselves at the threshold of a sea of ooze. In the middle of this sea is a small island with an odd cube and obelisk. In the final stage, the characters are to find pieces to a riddle to retrieve the amulet. The Faceless Lord, compelled to protect the amulet by the divine force of Dwurfater, has over the many millennia of his captivity created alternate realities and sub-planes linked together within his prison. He has hidden four stanzas of a riddle within these sub-planes. The four stanzas are necessary to open the amulet's resting place. You are encouraged to create these sub-planes, as they are a mechanism to expand the module significantly. Alternatively, you might forego the sub-planes and reach the ultimate conclusion — a direct confrontation with an avatar of the Faceless Lord. With or without the sub-planes, the adventure concludes at this point. The characters may leave the vault victorious with the demon's amulet, or they may become the latest liquefied victims of the Prince of Chaos.

Planar Travel

In *Chaos Rising*, the characters repeatedly enter and exit planes and travel through time. You can deal with this element in two ways. The first is to explain the travel as dimensional or planar travel, as is described in the module. In other words, the heroes travel from one plane of existence to an almost identical, but finite plane of existence that happens to exist in the past. This explanation avoids many of the consistency issues with time travel.

An alternate way of dealing with this matter is to explain the travel as true temporal relocation and time travel and ignore the demiplanes. In other words, the characters are actually traveling through time, and the interior of the Citadel and catacombs exist on the characters' home plane. This explanation may prove difficult, as many consistency issues arise. There is also the inevitable, "What happens if I kill my great-great-grandfather?" A good response is, "The inertia of time and destiny flattens the smallest ripples in time." Though this statement is rather meaningless, it is sufficiently ambiguous to quiet over-anxious questioners. The time stream does not abide a paradox.

A third option is not to explain the travel at all. The mystery of the situation allows the characters to come up with their own understanding of what is occurring. With any of these options, you should be able to tailor the concept to what your players will most enjoy.

Chronology of Events

Eons ago	The creation of the universe. The crafting of the vault by the Faceless Lord.
10,000 years ago	The vault crashes down on the characters' world and forms the Devil's Finger. Dwarves begin to revere it.
9,000 years ago	Dwurfater tricks the Faceless Lord and imprisons him in his vault. Construction begins on Dwurschmiede, the Citadel. Dwurfater creates two demiplanes to protect the key.
3,000 years ago	Orcus lays siege to the Citadel in an attempt to acquire the Faceless Lord's amulet for himself. The events of Stage Two take place.
1,300 years ago	The priest Giltz succeeds in destroying the last dwarves occupying the Citadel. He dies in battle.
1,200 years ago	The events of Stage Four take place.
1 year ago	Lord Raob learns of the amulet and its unspeakable power. He begins his quest to acquire it.
1 month ago	Lord Raob arrives at the Devil's Finger and begins to dig down toward the key. The characters' benefactor begins to learn of what Raob is trying to accomplish.
Today	The characters learn of Raob's plan from their benefactor. In the next two weeks, the events of Stage One and, later, Stage Three take place.
2 weeks from today	A blood moon rises and shows the door into the Citadel. The events of Stage Five take place.

PLAYING EFFECTIVE NPCS

This module includes a number of NPCs and NPC parties. A major NPC, of course, is the Faceless Lord. Raob and Sleeara are attempting to seize the amulet in the present; Lord Galm fights the forces of Orcus in the past. As well, numerous parties of "time-traveling" NPCs (as described in **Chapter Two**) await the characters.

Playing these NPCs effectively is a challenge, especially since the NPCs are not necessarily set encounters. Having completely new groups of NPCs jumping into the picture may not suit your game. If the adventure seems too hard for the characters, these NPCs allow you to scale the difficulty. For example, one change could be substituting Lord Raob with one of your campaign's reoccurring enemies. Another change could be not using an NPC party if the characters are bogged down in one of the Citadel levels. Furthermore, you could use your own NPC party that gains access to the Citadel upon learning what the characters are trying to accomplish.

Whether you use your own NPCs or those described in this adventure, understanding their motivations as well as their powers is important for playing them effectively with the encounters and events described in this adventure.

MAPS AND ENCOUNTER NUMBERING

Since the characters traverse the same "maps" twice in some circumstances, having a different map numbering and encounter system is necessary. Also, some of the encounters are not keyed to a specific place. Thus, the encounters are presented alphabetically with the chapter number (e.g., I-A). For the map references, the first letter indicates the specific map and the second is the Area number (i.e., A-1 refers to Map A and Area 1).

MODIFICATIONS TO THE ADVENTURE

Modifications to this adventure are not only recommended, they are expected. This adventure is written in such a way that it can take place on any world, in any campaign. These events could occur virtually anywhere.

A benefactor and evil demon are required. The benefactor, however, need not necessarily be good. An evil party could be hired by an evil deity to fetch the amulet for themselves. The demon could be the Faceless Lord or a long-forgotten demon of your own making. Likewise, the dwarves in this module could be any race that died out long ago or some other campaign-specific race.

Additionally, as was already mentioned, the NPCs are an easy target for modification to make the adventure more or less difficult. **Chapters Three** and **Five** are designed in such a way that you can tailor entire sections of encounters. In **Chapter Six**, you are expected to expand the sub-planes to provide strange and exciting locales for your campaign that the characters might not normally encounter.

One final note: Some encounters in this adventure are written with boxed, read-aloud description text. These descriptions are provided for your benefit. Whether you use the descriptions or not is up to you. Yet their purpose is to provide you with important pieces of dialogue, complex area descriptions, and ideas. The best descriptions for your players are yours. Consider the descriptions provided as helpful suggestions, not constraining requirements.

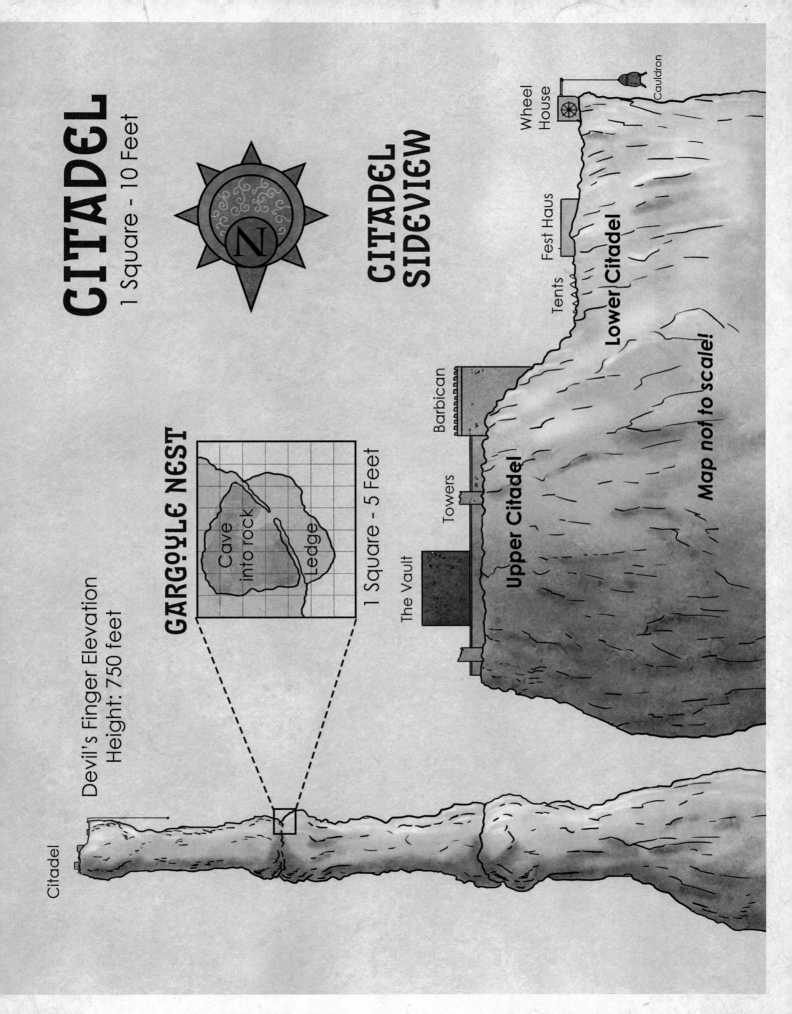

CITADEL

1 Square – 10 Feet

N

CITADEL SIDEVIEW

Cauldron

Wheel House

Fest Haus

Tents

Barbican

Towers

The Vault

Upper Citadel

Lower Citadel

Map not to scale!

GARGOYLE NEST

Cave into rock

Ledge

1 Square – 5 Feet

Devil's Finger Elevation
Height: 750 feet

Citadel

CHAPTER ONE: ASSAULT ON THE DEVIL'S FINGER

The adventure begins with the characters arriving at a valley within three miles of the Devil's Finger. How the characters arrive at this locale is up to you. Arriving at the remote location might be a difficult challenge for the characters; however, since time is of the essence (pun intended), having the benefactor described in the introduction spend the necessary funds to send the party via *teleport* to a grove of dead trees a few miles from the Devil's Finger might be easier. This adventure assumes that you have managed to get the characters to an area near the base of the Devil's Finger undetected by the agents of evil on the summit.

THE DEVIL'S FINGER

The Devil's Finger rises above one end of the valley. On all sides of the valley, dark mountains loom. Thunderstorms are common in the afternoon, and occasional strong winds have made the valley floor nearly barren. These strong winds mean creatures have disadvantage on ranged attack rolls and hamper those who attempt to fly (flying speed reduced by 25%).

SLEEARA'S WARNING CUBES

The *warning cubes* (See **Appendix A**) used by Sleeara are keyed to *detect magic*. Anyone carrying magical items and passing within 30 feet of a cube activates the *magic mouth*. The *magic mouth* begins to yell "ALERT!" repeatedly. A guard hears an activated cube on a successful DC 12 Wisdom (Perception) check.

The Devil's Finger resembles the bones of a humongous, three-jointed finger. It is more than 750 feet tall and made of granite. Two flat elevations are at the top of the Finger. The lower elevation has a number of rudimentary structures that are carved directly from the stone. These structures include the Fest Haus (**Encounter I-D**) and the Wheel House (**Encounter I-E**).

The Wheel House is a recent addition commissioned by Lord Raob. He placed an enormous cauldron at the end of a very thick rope connected to an immense wheel. The cauldron is large enough to accommodate five creatures. Lord Raob uses the Wheel House as an elevator to supply and move troops. Here and the landing area (**Encounter I-F**) see almost constant activity, making them two of the most heavily-guarded areas.

The higher elevation is the Citadel itself. Like buildings on the lower elevation, the Citadel is carved out of the Finger. A large barbican allows entry from the lower elevation to the higher elevation. In addition, within the barbican is the first magic portal — through which the characters must enter (**Encounter I-G**) in order to gain access to the Citadel's interior.

Visible in the center of the Citadel is the upper two-thirds of the massive obsidian cube that houses the demon's amulet. This cube is referred to as the vault. The Citadel flows around the vault, although the walls and towers that encircle the vault are devastated. The disrepair and collapsed walls and towers have in turn toppled the Citadel's two main levels, leaving rubble blocking nearly all of the passages. The dig (**Encounter I-C**) is slowly working through solid granite in an effort to reach the key. Until a week ago, Lord Raob made little progress. Now, Sleeara is personally overseeing the operation. Due to her motivational skills, the men have dug down nearly 100 feet. They have yet to discover any artifacts or remains from the "interior." Sleeara is starting to suspect the truth of the Citadel, that it is merely a façade.

Archers from Lord Raob's army watch the valley floor. During the day, the archers notice the characters far below on with a successful DC 17 Wisdom (Perception) check, even if the characters approach in the open. At night, seeing anything that is not lit is nearly impossible for the archers. If the characters use a light source, the DC to notice the approaching characters drops to 13.

ASCENT

The characters cannot teleport to the top of the Devil's Finger. Dwurfater infused the Citadel with magical energies that cause two effects that affect the adventure. The first effect is that contact with the Astral Plane is impossible; thus, spells such as *teleport* do not function around the Citadel. Second, spells cast within 100 feet around or on the Devil's Finger that contact other planes do not function unless the contact is to a non-evil plane. Thus, summoning spells targeting evil creatures fail; *gate* and divinination spells to evil planes also fail. Both magical enchantments are permanent and imbued in the stone.

Once at the base of the Devil's Finger, the characters may attempt to climb it. Each side of the Devil's Finger is smooth granite that flows in and out over the knobby protrusions or knuckles. Although natural edges can assist the characters in their ascent, the climb is still very difficult for non-thieves. Characters have a 40% chance of slipping and falling 3d6 feet for every 50 feet they climb; characters can make a DC 12 Dexterity saving throw to grab a protruding rock to arrest their fall or they take 3 (1d6) bludgeoning damage per 10 feet fallen. In addition, the gargoyles (**Encounter I-A**) make this method even harder.

INTRODUCTORY CHARACTERISTICS

Wandering Monsters: Patrols are infrequent beneath the Devil's Finger, as described above. This table is based on the party being at the top of the Devil's Finger. Check once every 10 minutes on 1d12:

1d12	Encounter
1	Sleeara and 4 **guards** (from **Encounter I-C**)
2	Lord Raob and 4 **guards** (from **Encounter I-D**)
3–5	1d4 **guards** (from **Encounter I-B**)
6	1d4 **gargoyles** (from **Encounter I-A**)
7–12	No encounter

Shielding: Spells cannot penetrate the vault (**Area A-7**). Nothing can damage or see beyond its jet-black obsidian walls. Ancient magical protections prevent anyone from traversing through the Astral Plane in and around the Citadel and the top of the Devil's Finger. Thus, astral travel and teleportation are impossible on, within, or 500 feet around the Devil's Finger. In addition, summoning and similar spells that target other planes function only if the target of the spell is not evil.

Detections: Characters detect strong evil and overwhelming magic from the vault (**Area A-7**) due to the presence of the Faceless Lord and his amulet. Also, the Devil's Finger itself radiates magical energies.

Standard Features: Unless otherwise noted, all doors are on a central pivot and made of stone.

Map Used: Map A: The Devil's Finger.

Characters may attempt to *fly*, *levitate*, or use some other magical means of ascent. Sleeara (**Encounter I-C**) placed a number of *warning cubes* (see **Appendix A**) on the perimeter of the army's base. These *warning cubes* are spaced evenly 100 feet apart on the perimeter. In between each *warning cube* are oil-fueled torches; although wind-resistant, they frequently blow out. A torch near where the party "arrives" has a 25% chance of being out.

Characters may also attempt to use the "cauldron-elevator" built by Lord Raob. See **Encounter I-F** for more details. This means of ascent, however, is very closely watched and most likely leads to detection.

Presuming the characters find a way to ascend to the Devil's Finger (most likely by *fly* and *invisibility*), they may have several encounters during their ascent. This initial set of encounters should be suspenseful but not overly difficult for the characters (unless Lord Raob's men spot them). They should feel that they are being challenged, but not taxed to their limits — that is for later.

ENCOUNTER I-A: GARGOYLES

Ten native **gargoyles** have taken up residence two-thirds of the way up the Devil's Finger. Their nest, little more than a small ledge in the granite, is located on the east side. This lair is more a repository of shiny objects and bits of wood than an actual nest, since the gargoyles sleep hanging on the Finger's surface during the day. More active at night, the gargoyles care little if the characters arrive on top of the Finger. However, while climbing the face of the formation, the characters are fair game to the gargoyles. The creatures' primitive minds believe that a new but dangerous food source has arrived.

The gargoyles lazily circle the Finger at dusk and dawn, creating an ominous image. During the day, they sleep with their wings folded over themselves, as still and silent as stone. Sleeping gargoyles are difficult to see. A climbing character may accidentally touch one of the gargoyles during the ascent of the upper portion of the citadel. If a character attempts to climb to the Citadel, he or she has a 20% chance of touching one of the creatures.

At night, the gargoyles fly, taking the occasional guard from above as a meal. The gargoyles like to linger near the perimeter torchlight and pull prey into the darkness between torches. Sleeara feeds the gargoyles occasionally by staking a member of Raob's army who "disappoints" her into the ground near the perimeter of the Citadel. The gargoyles are used to the strong winds by the Devil's Finger and are not affected by them.

Tactics: A single gargoyle that spots or is otherwise made aware of the party's presence gathers two other gargoyles before attacking. Thereafter, all three attempt to knock the "shiniest" party member (wearing gleaming armor, has a large gem, and so forth) to the ground below. The gargoyles are cowards at heart and do their best not to engage the characters directly. If the gargoyle nest is threatened, then the entire wing attacks the characters until a bargain is made (for more shiny objects) or one group or the other is dead.

The archers notice the characters if a battle ensues with the gargoyles with a successful DC 15 Wisdom (Perception) check. If spotted, the guards inform Sleeara, who engages the characters (as described in **Encounter I-C**). The archers are **guards** with AC 15 (chain shirt), no shield, and a longbow attack that is +3 to hit and does 5 (1d8 + 1) piercing damage.

Treasure: Stuffed into a large crack on a small three-foot ledge is the gargoyles' treasure. Numerous skulls, pieces of bone, and odd bits of metal are crammed into this crack. Far back in the space is a *+1 longsword* that requires five minutes of sorting and throwing items over the edge to acquire. Such actions, however, almost certainly grab the attention of the guards.

ATOP THE DEVIL'S FINGER

ENCOUNTER I-B: GUARDS

Lord Raob's army is 98 members strong on and around the Devil's Finger. These men are **guards** with AC 15 (chain shirt), no shield, and a longbow attack that is +3 to hit and does 5 (1d8 + 1) piercing damage. They are also manual laborers being used to dig down to the key. The guards work in three shifts: they dig for eight hours, rest for the next eight, then assume sentry duty during the final eight hours. These shifts rotate so that a crew is always digging, resting, and guarding. There are 30 men per crew.

At any one time, 30 men are working at the dig (**Area A-3**), 30 sleeping in tents outside of the Fest Haus (**Area A-4**), and 30 on guard. Of the men on guard, 15 patrol the perimeter in teams of two or three, 12 occupy the Wheel House (**Area A-5**), and the remaining three guards assist Sleeara in her motivational efforts at the dig (**Area A-3**).

The remaining eight guards are sergeants who command the men and serve as Raob's personal guards. They use the statistics of a **guard** with the following changes:

- They have 39 (6d8 + 12) hit points.
- They have a longsword attack: +4 to hit, 6 (1d8 + 2) slashing damage.
- They have a longbow attack: +4 to hit, 6 (1d8 + 2) piercing damage.
- Their Challenge Rating is 1 (200 XP).

Tactics: If a "credible enemy" is spotted, a large bell rings out at the Fest Haus. This bell was taken from a church as plunder and put to use as a warning device. A credible enemy is one that presents a potential threat to the dig, Sleeara, or Raob. If the general alarm is sounded, the army springs into action. After 1d4+2 minutes, the guards at the dig arrive at the Fest Haus. The guards who were asleep pick up their weapons and are ready to engage after 1d6 + 2 minutes. After 10 minutes, the dig guards are ready for battle. The guards at the Wheel House remain in position to defend the cauldron elevator.

The guards' tactics are simple: charge and kill. The sergeants lead sorties against the enemy, striking at the largest target first. If casualties drop their numbers to 50%, the guards flee to regroup. Sleeara and Raob's tactics are listed separately in **Encounters I-C** and **I-D**.

Each guard has black enameled chainmail, a white cape, a spear, a longbow, 30 arrows, and 1d4 gems (worth 1d10 x 10 gp each). Each sergeant has black enameled chainmail, a red cape, a longsword, a longbow, 30 arrows, and 1d4 gems (worth 1d10 x 10 gp each).

ENCOUNTER I-C: SLEEARA AND THE DIG (AREA A-1)

The dig is near the barbican's west tower. Digging down into the tough granite, Raob and his men are slowly inching their way toward where they presume the key lies. The men work in a long line, passing rocks to one another and eventually depositing them on a large mound that is growing outside of the barbican.

Sleeara and 3 **guards** oversee this operation. The guards have AC 15 (chain shirt), no shield, and a longbow attack that is +3 to hit and does 5 (1d8 + 1) piercing damage. Sleeara has the statistics of a **death mage** (see **Appendix B**) with the following changes:

- She has a *staff of power.*
- She has AC 18 (*robe of the archmagi* and *ring of protection*).
- She has a spell save DC 17 and a +9 to spell attacks due to her robe.
- Her Challenge Rating is 11 (7,200 XP).

The guards are callous, brutal, and quick to whip their fellows at any opportunity. One day, a guard may be whipped, and the next he is the one holding the whip. Each guard has 1d4 gems (each worth 1d10 x 10 gp).

Sleeara stalks around the dig, making sure the men are properly motivated. She has executed a few men for failure to meet her harsh expectations. Some of these men were staked out for the gargoyles, and one was thrown over the ledge. Sleeara's motivation is to press the men to complete the task before the end of the fortnight when the blood moon rises. Note: Sleeara hides her spellbook in her room in the Fest Haus.

Sleeara is an overambitious brat. She believes she is vastly more powerful than she really is and goes to great lengths to prove her "superiority." Early in her short career, she fell in with Lord Raob, who at the time went under the name Raob Darkly. Although she no longer fancies him as much as she once did, he is still deeply infatuated with her. Sleeara, of course, has used his feelings to her advantage. She disposed of all competitors, such as a priestess of Demogorgon, and has solidified her position by discovering the history of the demon's amulet through her necromantic studies. Sleeara is likely to inquire about the characters' *portal rune* (see **Appendix A**) tattoo if they are captured. If possible, she tries to copy and use it. Sleeara goes to any length to impress someone, because doing so impresses herself.

ENCOUNTER I-D: RAOB AND THE FEST HAUS (AREA A-2)

The aboveground Fest Haus is a long and narrow structure that the dwarves once used presumably to host celebrations outside of the Citadel. It is made entirely of stone and has a simple opening as its entrance. Above the entrance, in an ancient dialect of Dwarvish, an inscription reads "Festival House." The roof on the Fest Haus is of poor construction and tends to leak during rain. The interior of the structure is bare, except for the items Raob has moved into it.

Lord Raob Blackenheart uses the statistics of a **commander** (see **Appendix B**) with the following changes:

- He wields a *+2 flail* with which he is +9 to hit and does 10 (1d8 + 6) bludgeoning damage.
- He has AC 21 (*+1 plate armor*, shield)
- Raob uses the Fest Haus as his base of operations. In fact, he pitched an elaborate red pavilion in the structure's center. Raob and Sleeara sleep in this pavilion (apart, much to Raob's chagrin). Raob's personal guards also sleep in the Fest Haus, but outside of the pavilion. They use the statistics of a **guard** with the following changes:
- They have 39 (6d8 + 12) hit points.
- They have a longsword attack: +4 to hit, 6 (1d8 + 2) slashing damage.
- They have a longbow attack: +4 to hit, 6 (1d8 + 2) piercing damage.
- Their Challenge Rating is 1 (200 XP)

Each guard has 1d4 gems (each worth 1d10 x 10 gp).

The pavilion itself has three "rooms." Two are the sleeping chambers, and one is a common area where Raob eats, dresses, and contemplates how he will rule the world once he obtains the demon's amulet. A large map of the known world is on the floor, with many of the country's names changed to "Skullcracker," "Raobland," or "Sleeara Hold." The map has a base value of 1,000 gp. There are also silk pillows, an incense burner, and a small mirror; together, these furnishings are worth 300 gp.

In Raob's sleeping chamber is an armor stand, a king-sized bed (which the guards still grumble about hauling up the Devil's Finger), and a stuffed bear missing a button eye hidden under the bed. The chamber also contains a chest, which is trapped with a poisoned arrow. The trap can be found with a successful DC 15 Intelligence (Investigation) check and disarmed with a successful DC 15 Dexterity check with thieves' tools. If the chest is opened without disarming the trap, the creature opening the chest must make a DC 15 Dexterity saving throw, taking 44 (8d10) poison damage on a failure or half as much damage on a success. Inside the chest are 10 platinum bars worth 1,000 gp each, a large ruby worth 250 gp, and an ancient cloth map showing the location of the Devil's Finger in the nearby mountain range.

Fully armed, Raob is an imposing sight. He wears black enameled full plate armor with a large helm bearing metal eagle's wings. A large open hand with an eye in the palm — Raob's symbol — is painted in gold on his breastplate. He usually has his helm open so he can bark orders at his men, showing his yellow teeth and grizzly beard.

Raob Blackenheart, a self-proclaimed lord with no ties to nobility, has the mewling personality of a four-year-old. Although clearly an adult, his basic motivations are similar to a young child's; he is moody, he loves to satisfy himself and his needs, and he hates anyone who stands in the way. He has a deep infatuation with Sleeara. This is the reason why he allows her to command him. Yet Raob may grow tired of her one day and eliminate her, as he has eliminated other concubines. Finally, Raob is a force of destruction. He is very large (standing 6 feet 5 inches tall and weighing over 250 pounds), with jet-black hair and a long black beard. His eyes dart around the room when anyone talks to him, as if he is always wary of an attack. He wields absolute control over his men due to the awe he strikes in them with his prowess in battle.

In Sleeara's sleeping chamber are black silk blankets and a pillow. Underneath this bedroll is her spellbook. The spellbook contains all of the spells Sleeara currently has memorized; you can include additional spells as you see fit. The bedroll was a gift from Raob. A *warning cube* (see **Appendix A**) also rests on a small locked crate. The crate has been secured with a lightning trap, though nothing is inside the crate because Sleeara always carries her possessions with her. The trap can be found with a successful DC 15 Intelligence (Investigation) check while examining the crate and disarmed with a successful DC 15 Dexterity check with thieves' tools. If the crate is opened without disarming the trap, it unleashes a 50-foot-long five-foot-wide lightning bolt in the direction of the creature opening the crate. All creatures in that area must make a DC 15 Dexterity saving throw, taking 21 (6d6) lightning damage on a failure and half as much damage on a success. The blast destroys the crate. The crate can be unlocked with a successful DC 10 Dexterity check with thieves' tools or broken open with a successful DC 12 Strength check.

Tactics: Although he is fearful of magic and hates wizards (excluding Sleeara), Raob usually charges into the thick of any combat and calls out challenges to the largest of the enemy. While a few large battles have gone differently, Raob personally has never lost a challenge. With the cliff nearby, Raob may try to push someone over it to eliminate him or her. No tactic is beneath him. Raob commands his men as described in **Encounter II-B**.

ENCOUNTER I-E: THE WHEEL HOUSE AND LANDING AREA (AREA A-3)

As previously mentioned, the Wheel House is a new building on the lower elevation on top of the Devil's Finger. It is a shanty-like wood structure crafted of odd pieces of brushwood hastily gathered far below.

The Wheel House hangs slightly over the cliff's edge. Inside the structure is a large and well-crafted wheel that functions as a spool for a very thick rope. The rope is connected by way of a pulley to a gigantic iron cauldron. Together, the entire system acts like an elevator.

At all times, 3 **guards** — with AC 15, no shield, and a longbow attack that is +3 to hit and does 5 (1d8 + 1) piercing damage — are far below watching the landing area; at night, they use torches to provide light for this operation. Above, the remaining eight guards work in shifts to turn the wheel, moving it around in a great circle. Operating the wheel requires at least two characters to make a successful Open Doors check; it usually takes three to four guards to turn the wheel. The remaining guards watch outside, always alert and present when the cauldron reaches the top. The cauldron weighs 200 pounds. If for any reason the cauldron is let loose and falls on top of someone, it deals 7 (2d6) bludgeoning damage for every 10 feet it plummets, to a maximum of 70 (20d6). Each guard carries 2 gems (each worth 1d10 x 10 gp).

NEW SPELL: PORTAL RUNE

A *portal rune* spell (See **Appendix A**) tattoos a portal key directly onto the recipient's flesh. A *portal rune* is usually tattooed on the back of the neck in order to prevent someone from hacking off a limb and attempting to use the rune. Granted, chopping off someone's head might accomplish the same task with a precision cut. An unwilling target can resist the *portal rune* spell with a successful saving throw.

In **Chaos Rising**, the *portal rune* to the Citadel is the Dwarvish rune for the fire that fuels Dwurfater's forge. This rune is recognized by most of the dwarves encountered in **Chaos Rising** as a holy symbol of good.

The use of a *portal rune* in the appropriate portal to which it is keyed is instantaneous and individual. Any other being carried by the recipient of a *portal rune* does not transport. Due to the ritual used, the *portal rune* is permanent and does not disappear by use of the portal. A *portal rune* is keyed only to one portal. Also, a *portal rune* functions within an *antimagic field* because it is merely a trigger for magic beyond the field — namely, the portal itself, which draws magic from planar effects beyond the scope of the field.

In **Chaos Rising**, the *portal rune* allows the characters to access only the Citadel's interior (i.e., through the upper portal). They must convince King Galm (in **Chapter Three**) to grant them the necessary *portal rune* to access the catacombs.

ENCOUNTER I-F: OUTER BARBICAN (AREA A-4)

Like most of the Citadel, the outer barbican is nearly completely dilapidated. The great stone ceiling and towers are collapsed and crumbling. The Citadel is distinguished from the Devil's Finger because it has a brushed and smooth structure. Yet the Citadel has no visible entrance, except in the courtyard around the vault and the barbican.

The entrance to the Citadel through the barbican was formerly a 30-foot-wide entryway. This way has since been blocked by rubble. The dig nearby is concentrating on the west tower (**Area A-1**). The north tower is accessible from a collapsed wall on the north side. This collapsed wall has created a hole through which the characters could climb and enter the barbican.

Once inside, the characters enter a passageway in the north tower. The upper floors are destroyed. A number of rooms are in the north tower, but they are empty, with only bits of wood and dust (this area was once a barracks). In a corner room is a hole in the floor that has larger stones around its perimeter. This is not a privy, but rather access to a lower storage area. Through this storage area is the archway that gives the characters access to the Citadel (**Encounter I-J**). No guards patrol here.

ENCOUNTER I-G: THE VAULT (AREA A-5)

The vault is a very large cube of obsidian, each side flawless and mirror-like black stone. Around the edges is a crater that was smoothed by the Citadel's architects. Only 50 feet of the cube is visible from the surface, but it extends another 16 feet into the granite. Only the key provides access into the vault, as described in **Chapter Six**.

Around the vault is a low, five-foot-high wall that forms a pentagram. The wall is made of individual stones and has crumbled and fallen in places. Each individual stone has the same Dwarvish rune on it; the rune reads "evil" and is non-magical.

There is no way into the Citadel itself, since it is a façade. The outer Citadel was dug out of the granite below. Theoretically, a party could blast its way down 40 to 50 feet, as Raob did; however, this strategy is mere folly and a waste of valuable time. The vault radiates strong evil and overwhelming magic.

ENCOUNTER I-H: THE UPPER CITADEL (AREA A-6)

The old remnants of the Citadel's towers and walls barely stand. The wall was made of individual bricks of granite that fit together without mortar. This is an example of the unique and marvelous structure that the dwarves created. When it was first built, the wall formed a circle and was 50 feet high and five feet wide. Now, large holes show in the wall where the bricks were toppled over.

The large, 70-foot-tall towers are also nearly all collapsed. Some are mere rings, and at least one retains part of its crenulations (like the wall, it was made of granite bricks). The party can explore the towers, but the only entrance to the Citadel below is through the barbican (**Encounter I-F**).

ENCOUNTER I-I: OUTER BUILDINGS (AREA A-7)

Like the Fest Haus, these buildings were made of large slabs of granite stacked together. Whatever occupied the interior has long since turned to dust or been removed. The original purpose of these buildings is unknown.

The buildings are somewhat unstable. Combat or some other such activity has a 10% chance of toppling a structure. If this event occurs, a character must succeed on a DC 12 Dexterity saving throw or take 10 (3d6) bludgeoning damage from falling rubble.

ENCOUNTER I-J: ENTRY TO CHAOS

The corner room of the lower barbican leads to a great archway that is carved with numerous ancient Dwarvish runes inlaid with brass. Rubble and rock lie five feet beyond the archway. Near the archway, the ribcage of a dwarf is propped up against the wall, the rusted blade of a dagger lying within it. A few rats make their home in a corner rubble pile.

The characters can activate the portal merely by walking through it if they wear the *portal rune* (see **Appendix A**). Anyone else present described in **Chapter One** — other than Sleeara — would be too perplexed or frightened to attempt to follow the characters. If anyone does and fails to possess a *portal rune*, he or she is transported through time and considered lost (the exact location is up to you, although a time when the characters' home planet has long since been destroyed — and thus the unfortunate is transported to a vacuum — or when the entire planet is covered in primal molten rock are good choices).

If Sleeara is secretly observing the characters, she may immediately realize the truth of the archway and the necessary rune. If she saw such a rune on a character's neck, she is likely to follow them (as described in **Chapter Two**) once she inscribes and tattoos the rune on herself.

When the characters move through the archway, they are instantly transported to the "Siege of Orcus" in **Chapter Three**. The rubble is gone, the area is changed, and the silence is soon broken by the sounds of Dwarvish battle cries resonating through the halls.

If the characters look through the archway back toward the direction from which they entered, they see blackness. In other words, when standing in the archway during the "Siege of Orcus," the characters do not see the broken stone and collapsed barbican from which they entered. Instead, they see inky blackness and apparent nothingness.

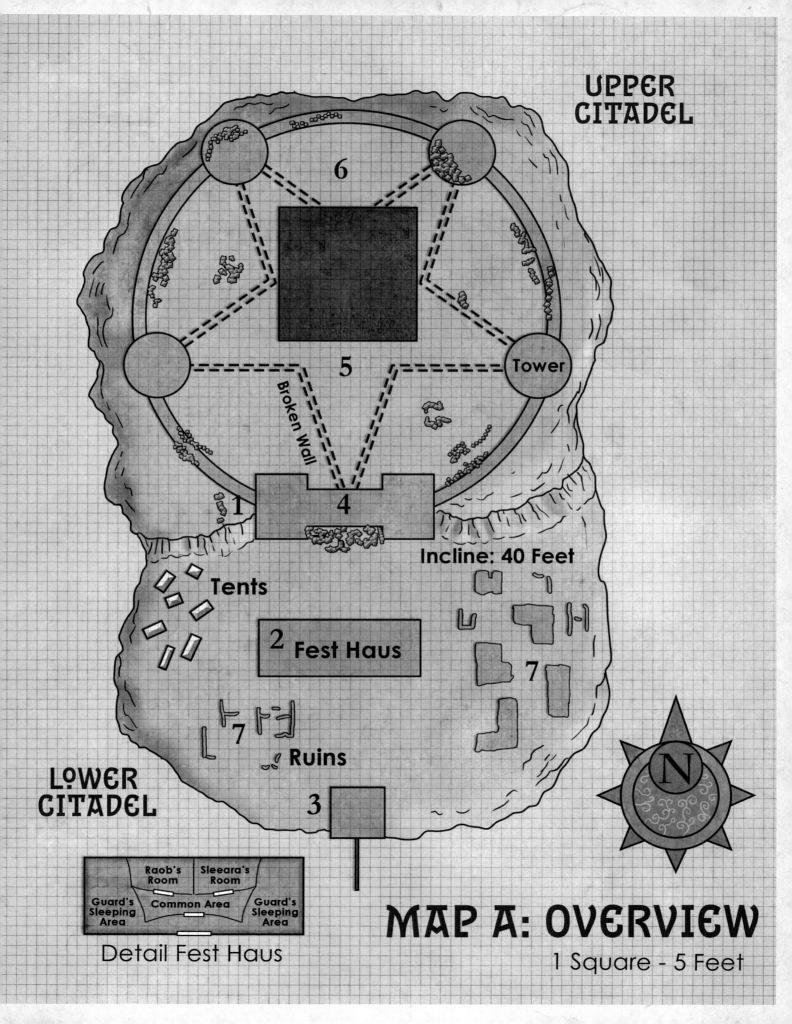

UPPER CITADEL

6

5

Broken Wall

Tower

4

1

Incline: 40 Feet

Tents

2 Fest Haus

7

7

Ruins

LOWER CITADEL

3

	Raob's Room	Sleeara's Room	
Guard's Sleeping Area	Common Area		Guard's Sleeping Area

Detail Fest Haus

N

MAP A: OVERVIEW

1 Square - 5 Feet

CHAPTER TWO: THE CITADEL

Chaos. Total chaos. This is the path the characters select. This is the path you must arbitrate. What follows is bizarre, unusual, and — with preparation by you — thoroughly fun.

This chapter first explains a general outline for the characters' adventures in the Citadel. Next is a description of and motivations for "competing" NPC parties. Although whether to include these parties in *Chaos Rising* is up to you, doing so is ultimately a wise idea. Finally, this chapter includes a description of the Citadel's two levels. Since the Citadel is mostly unchanged, the two times the characters move through it, these descriptions are provided here. Further specifics are explained in the pertinent chapters, **Chapter Three: Descent — The Siege of Orcus** and **Chapter Five: Ascent — Necromantic Dreams**.

A JOURNEY THROUGH CHAOS

In Stage Two, the characters time travel. They leave the present and enter the Citadel through the upper archway. In doing so, they enter an alternate demiplane that occupies only two levels of the Citadel. The laws of physics on the demiplane are the same as the characters' home plane, and time advances at the same rate. In other words, the dwarves on the demiplane age and die the same as dwarves on the home plane. Practically nothing is different except that the barbican portal can access only the demiplane.

Once through the archway, the characters are thrust into the middle of a battle. Orcus has persuaded an evil dwarven priest, Kinst, to open a special gate into the Citadel, bypassing all its defenses. The dwarven high priest, Usis, received a vision two days before the attack. In this vision, Usis saw demons devouring dwarves within the Citadel. Usis warned King Galm, the Clan Flammeaxte leader, and together they prepared for the assault.

During the preparations, Usis fell into a coma due to Kinst poisoning him one day before the characters' arrival. No one suspects Kinst and believes that the poisoning is the work of demons. Undeterred, King Galm prepares patrols and believes that the demons might arrive through the upper portal.

As the characters enter the upper portal, they are met by a group of guardian dwarves. The characters must do some quick explaining and possibly show the *portal rune* (see **Appendix A**) they used to gain access to the Citadel. If the characters gain these dwarves' trust, they are escorted to King Galm, who then interrogates them. Galm wants to know why they are in the Citadel and how they gained access; he should at best be skeptical during this conversation.

Toward the end of the conversation, King Galm is alerted that demons are within the Citadel and running amok. Galm immediately wants to join the battle. His advisors restrain him, however, and warn that if he should fall and the demons acquire his *portal rune*, the enemy will gain access to the catacombs. An advisor to Galm — or perhaps Galm himself — suggests that the characters take care of the threat as a sign of their good intentions. This suggestion triggers a whirlwind of events that is more fully described in **Chapter Four**.

Assuming that the characters persuade King Galm to give them the *portal rune* to the catacombs, which might be inscribed by the priests of Dwurfater from the rune on the back of Galm's neck, they enter the catacombs' demiplane. Like the Citadel, the catacombs are similar physically and temporally to the characters' home plane. Yet the catacombs the characters enter are at a different era than the "Siege of Orcus": they are in the present — or, the same time that the characters left behind when they entered the Citadel.

Once in the catacombs, the characters must overcome guardians and traps to retrieve the key. The key is unusual in many respects. One such property is that the key suppresses magic as per an *antimagic field*. This property does not prevent the characters from using the *portal key* to return from the catacombs and re-enter the Citadel's demiplane. The *portal key*, as explained in **Chapter One**, actually functions in an *antimagic field*. Yet it does not return the characters to the time of Galm, where they are likely heroes. Instead, the *portal key* takes them to "Necromantic Dreams" (see **Chapter Five**).

In "Necromantic Dreams," the Citadel is completely abandoned. A priest (Giltz, now a dark custodian, see **Appendix B**) led his army into the Citadel in search of the key. While his army was successful, Giltz died in a suicide effort by the last defenders. These events occurred more than 100 years before the characters arrive the via the lower portal.

The remnants of Giltz's army, the undead, roam the Citadel. The entire complex is dark and seems barely disturbed; thrones sit empty and benches gather dust. Although the Citadel was attacked, the interior is oddly in the same condition as when the characters left the "Siege of Orcus" … as if the dwarves suddenly disappeared and were replaced with undead. The characters must make their way through this nightmarish Citadel and return to their home plane through the upper archway. Unfortunately for them, Giltz has other plans.

In both the "Siege of Orcus" and the return trip through "Necromantic Dreams," the characters cannot leave the demiplane without going through the upper or lower portal. Any attempt to leave the upper or lower levels via teleportation or similar means is stunted by the Citadel's magical wards. The Citadel was designed with magical protections imbued into the fabric of the structure or plane to stop any evil-aligned entity from entering it via a *gate* or other magical means (note, however, that Orcus overcame these wards by using a specially-crafted magic item). *Teleport* and similar spells *within* the levels are permissible. In other words, the characters may teleport between rooms they are familiar with inside the Citadel. They cannot teleport outside the Citadel. Furthermore, the Citadel's demiplane is infused with dwarven magical energy that repairs any attempt to break through the Citadel's walls.

Overcoming Giltz, the characters return to their home plane. Here, the final chapter begins. The characters discover that while they entered the demiplanes of the Citadel and the catacombs, time moved very shortly in the outside world (perhaps one day for every four the characters experienced) — giving them time to deal with Raob (if necessary) and use the key when the blood moon rises. With preparation, you can easily play these chaotic events as described above.

COMPETING NPCs (TIME TRAVELERS)

Recommended, but not necessary, is the addition of an unexpected challenge. The characters might assume that they will meet guardians and traps. They might not foresee others seeking to take the key.

These competing NPCs might enter the Citadel during the "Siege of Orcus" or "Necromantic Dreams" and challenge the characters. This challenge could be to beat the characters into the catacombs during the "Siege of Orcus", or it could be to take the key while the characters are in "Necromantic Dreams."

Below are three groups of NPCs and a single NPC "operative": the Brotherhood of Ooze, the Cabal of the Beard, the Silvereyes, and the nefarious mercenary Imbo the Undying. With the exception of the Cabal, any of these NPCs may be inserted in either the "Siege of Orcus" or "Necromantic Dreams."

Use these groups with caution. To be certain, this adventure is not easy. Thus, the NPCs should be inserted with a specific plan in mind, as each group employs different tactics.

For simplicity's sake, using only a couple of the NPC groups in either time period might prove more effective. For example, use Imbo the Undying during the "Siege of Orcus" and the Brotherhood of the Ooze along with the Cabal of the Beard during "Necromantic Dreams." Still, a fun challenge might be to arbitrate two such groups at the same time against the characters. The characters might find themselves allying with one against another. Switching allegiances or joining together against a common foe such as Kinst, these NPCs provide unique challenges for the party beyond the norm.

When introducing the NPCs, having the NPCs fight the denizens of whichever era you place them in "behind the scenes" may be too difficult. Instead, simply place the NPCs in a set locale and consider that they fought or made their way there by eliminating other creatures not described. This way, the NPCs become a living entity from the encounter point forward in harrying the characters and their quest.

Also, with the exception of the Brotherhood of Ooze, the NPCs are not illogical or dim. They are some of the finest warriors, priests, and wizards who, just like the characters, are after a prize of considerable value. They might leave the Citadel and return later (such as leave in the "Siege of Orcus" and return in "Necromantic Dreams"). Or they might leave and attempt to ambush the characters in the characters' real world. Also, these NPCs could ambush the characters after the events of this adventure take place as the characters attempt to return the demon's amulet to their benefactor. Finally, these NPCs might even become a reoccurring enemy in your campaign world long after *Chaos Rising*.

THE CABAL OF THE BEARD

The Cabal of the Beard is a group of dwarven guardians established in the Citadel hundreds of years after the "Siege of Orcus." These guardians believe that King Galm of old made a horrendous mistake in allowing the characters to enter the catacombs. Over the years, the cabal grew strong and opposed the ruling king. Successful in their coup, the cabal sends Bertram and company through time to take the key from the characters. Interestingly, the rise of the cabal is directly responsible for the success of Kinst later in time owing to the divisions it caused within Clan Flammeaxte.

The Cabal of the Beard should be used only in "Necromantic Dreams." The cabal is perplexed that the Citadel is in ruins and is only discovering the truth that the dwarves have all perished. This realization causes much sadness to the cabal, which, although lawful good, is likely to blame the characters for the death of their people.

The leader of the cabal party is Lord Bertram auth'Tanak, a **captain** (see **Appendix B**) with the following changes:

- He has a *+1 battleaxe* with which he is +8 to hit and does 9 (1d8 + 5) slashing damage.
- He has AC 20 (*dwarven plate* armor).
- He has a *potion of animal friendship*, a *potion of growth*, a *potion of heroism*, and a *potion of speed*.

Description: Bertram appears as a squat suit of pristine armor with a tuft of red whiskers billowing from his chin. He is never without his family's great heirloom: a battleaxe dating back to the time of the Citadel's founding. He is harsh and is incredibly bigoted against all non-dwarves.

Background: Bertram is the direct descendant of a coward who hid during the "Siege of Orcus." This dwarf was so consumed by guilt that he swore that one day a descendent of his would make up for his cowardice. Bertram knows this story and is fanatical about protecting the Citadel.

Motivation: Bertram had little interest in the cabal until he received the vision from Dwurfater. As an elder of the cabal, he is a zealot through and through. Bertram has trained his group hard and accepts nothing less than total victory.

DEITY — DWURFATER

Name: Dwurfater, Father of Dwarves
Status: Dwurfater is the father of all dwarves. He eternally works his forge to create dwarves to populate the universe so that they can glorify him with works of mithral and steel.
Pantheon: Dwarven
Alignment: Lawful Good
Spheres of Influence: Creation, Earth, Good, Strength
Symbol: Hammer and anvil
Garb: Armor of mithral or steel
Favored Weapon: Warhammer
Typical Worshippers: Dwarves (good-aligned)

Another dedicated member of the cabal is Kunuld, a **preacher** (see **Appendix B**) with the following changes:

- She has AC 20 (plate, shield)
- She wields a *+1 warhammer*: +7 to hit, 8 (1d8 + 4) bludgeoning damage.
- She has a *spell scroll* of *raise dead* and a *potion of healing*.

Description: Kunuld is a devotee of Dwurfater. Like Bertram, she wears gleaming plate armor. Beneath the armor, she has a pleasant, plump face and a smiling disposition. Kunuld is a kind person but does not flinch from a chance to smite evil.

Background: Kunuld was born into the priesthood of Dwurfater. She has dedicated her life to his cause and is delighted that Bertram selected her for this holy mission.

Motivation: Kunuld worries that Bertram's fervor will be his undoing. She is levelheaded and will be one of the first to attempt to parley with the characters if possible.

Also in the cabal is Teera auth'Narak, a **burglar** (see **Appendix B**) with the following changes:

- She has AC 16 (*+1 leather armor*)
- She wields a *+1 quarterstaff*: +8 to hit, 8 (1d6 + 5) bludgeoning damage or 9 (1d8 + 5) bludgeoning damage if used with two hands.
- She has a *ring of resistance* (fire).

Description: Teera is a thin dwarf with flowing, raven-colored hair. She almost always has a smile on her face and loves the thrill of adventure. Teera tends to annoy others because of her shrill voice and laughter. She wears oversized (elf-sized) leather armor that she keeps well-oiled. Also, she uses an unusual weapon for a dwarf: the quarterstaff.

Background: Teera always longed to leave the Citadel and explore the outside world. Yet her father prohibited such wanderlust. As a youth, the elves — the dwarves' ancient enemy — fascinated her. Although she never met one, reading about their carefree lifestyle and troublemaking suited her. Bertram was smitten with her and still bears feelings for her. Teera has always thought of Bertram as stuffy, but she is very loyal to him.

Motivation: Teera lives for adventure. She secretly fancies herself an elf soul (a being with the soul of the elf, but who is actually something else). She sticks with Bertram as long as the arrangement suits her; however, if a situation gets very dangerous or deadly, she may sneak off.

Finally, **Auran** fills out the cabal. He is a **captain** (see **Appendix B**) with the following changes:

- He has AC 17 (chain mail, *cloak of protection*)
- He wields a *+1 scythe* with statistics of a glaive: +8 to hit, 10 (1d10 + 5) slashing damage.
- He has 12 *+1 bolts* for his crossbow.

Description: Auran is an incredibly hairy dwarf. With the exception of his cheekbones, nose, and eyes, Auran has brown hair covering his entire face. He rarely speaks, but when he does, he usually barks out insults and threats. He wears a raggedy old cloak over armor that squeaks a bit too much. He is very fond of his scythe ("Cutting the chaff of life" is a favorite expression), and his shield emblazoned with Dwurfater's symbol (a hammer and anvil).

Background: Auran is an old friend of Bertram's, but he does not trust the other dwarf's leadership. He was regimented to learn to be a guard while his noble-born friend Bertram was privileged to learn better fighting tactics. In addition to his station in the Citadel during the time from which they came, Auran feels everyone picks on him as he had a very difficult childhood.

Motivation: Auran is a very bitter dwarf with little patience for folly. Like Bertram, he is secretly infatuated with Teera, which explains how he can stand her "shenanigans." Auran does not trust any of the bigger people (humans, elves, orcs) he has read about, and due to the stories he has read, he usually displays an open disdain for the smaller people (halflings). Auran is likely to lead the group if Bertram is killed.

All of the cabal have a *portal rune* (see **Appendix A**) to enter the upper hall. Instead of taking them to the outer world, it returns them to their time era.

Although Bertram is arrogant and foolish, the rest of these dwarves are not likely to risk their lives fighting a foe that they recognize as having good intentions. Thus, a parley is possible, especially if a good-aligned dwarf leads or appears to lead the party.

Encountering the cabal is an excellent opportunity for the characters to gain allies to help them defeat some of the more difficult foes in "Necromantic Dreams." These dwarves are skeptical and have large chips on their shoulders (for dwarves); they are likely to attack, retreat, and assess the situation. An initial encounter will

not likely lead to death, as far as the cabal is concerned. What the characters do is another story.

If the party does not include a dwarf, the characters may have difficulty explaining why they are carrying a 500-pound platinum anvil. The cabal, like almost all dwarves of the Citadel at any time, has never seen the key and is unlikely to recognize it as such. If the characters tell the cabal that the anvil is the key, however, a battle to the death is very likely.

Even with a dwarf in the party, unless the words "holy quest" or some similar dire reason is quickly explained, the cabal may become hostile. A good way for the characters to gain the cabal's assistance is to implore their help and ask for guidance through the Citadel. The cabal may view this as a redeeming opportunity and be happy to oblige.

The cabal is immediately hostile if the characters are in the company of the Brotherhood of Ooze. The cabal knows little of the brotherhood but can tell immediately that they serve chaos and the Faceless Lord, the defeated foe of Dwurfater.

The following description details the cabal. Its use is a matter of your discretion.

This entire room is full of rubble, trash, and splintered wood. Where once the dwarves of the Citadel lived is now destruction and decay.

Four dwarves stand among the junk. One wears a dwarven-sized suit of silvery plate armor that has an otherworldly glow from the magical light his group is using. He has a tuft of red whiskers below a full helm and a mask of a jolly dwarf face with the wearer's beard and lower chin uncovered. The dwarf holds a large battleaxe. Next to him stands a shorter dwarf in the same style of armor. Obviously a female, she presses her lips together as if ready to blurt something out; she holds an oversized warhammer with a gleaming silver head. Behind them, balanced on a plank of wood sticking out of the junk pile, is a very thin and raven-haired dwarf, smiling broadly. This dwarf begins to snicker, slowly twirling a quarterstaff.

Finally, at the base of the junk pile is a filthy dwarf wearing a tattered cloak over rust-spotted armor. He has a large scar across his face that ends in a gap between his teeth. His bristly red hair and beard are unkempt. He hefts a large scythe and braces as if to swing it.

The first dwarf says to you, "The deceivers! Come, me brudders, let us have our taste of sweet vengeance!"

Tactics: If combat becomes necessary, the cabal springs into action. Bertram drinks a *potion of growth* and immediately bellows challenges at the enemy. He then engages them. Auran attempts to move to the back of the enemies' position and uses his massive scythe on enemy casters, hopefully flanking the frontlines of the enemy fighters. Teera fires her crossbow while protecting Kunuld. Kunuld's tactics change depending on the encounter, though her primary role is to heal and support her comrades.

THE BROTHERHOOD OF THE OOZE

The Brotherhood of the Ooze is a bumbling and absentminded group dedicated to the worship of absolute chaos. Sickly and vile, a Brother of the Ooze makes his way through life seeding chaos wherever he roams. A Brother is the personification of chaos. He tries to bring disorder to order, disharmony to harmony, and is thoroughly evil.

Drawing both men and women, the Brotherhood of the Ooze has no sexism save the name. The Brothers of the Ooze are mostly clerics and some wizards. They learn of the art of chaos, and this path leads them to the name of the Faceless Lord.

DEITY — THE FACELESS LORD

Name: Jubilex, The Faceless Lord, The Prince of Slime
Status: The Faceless Lord is a demon prince sometimes worshipped as a deity. He is chaos personified. Also thoroughly evil, he strives to sew chaos and discord among the planes. He is most often depicted as an enormous and amorphous blob that spews forth foul and sickly slimes of many colors.
Alignment: CE
Pantheon: Abyssal Horde, Castorhagi, Cthonic
Spheres of Influence: Chaos, Evil, Water
Symbol: An amulet portraying an amorphous mass covered in eyes or a splatter of paint with an eye drawn in the center
Garb: Filthy rags
Favored Weapon: Morningstar (called a "pulper" by the faithful)
Typical Worshippers: Insane humans, lepers, intelligent oozes
Stats for an **Avatar of Jubilex** are given in **Appendix B**.

Brothers of the Ooze cling together. They are outcasts, the downtrodden, and those with darkened hearts. Although a Brother might be found in any locale, the group recruits in beggar quarters in large cities and in deep underground temples where they perform horrific rites and delight in the perfection of chaos — the oozes.

Through the direction of their master, the Faceless Lord, they preach and chant litanies on the virtues of sludge and muck. Slime is chaos perfected to the Brotherhood: it is ever-flowing, ever-moving, and its effects are unpredictable.

One way you may use the brotherhood is to make them comical, as per the below description. A group that is chanting about the glory of sludge while sliding about on their own slime is humorous in its own way. The humor vanishes, however, when these comical antics end in a deadly encounter.

The brotherhood made a pilgrimage to the Devil's Finger to discover more about their obscure religion. Since the Faceless Lord's imprisonment within the vault, his powers as a deity have greatly diminished. Although the Faceless Lord is faintly aware of the brotherhood and how pathetic they are, he believes that they could also be his salvation. In a vision, he sent the brotherhood the image of the *portal rune* (see **Appendix A**). After a week of debate, someone figured out what the *portal rune* meant, and the brotherhood entered the Citadel.

If the characters have the key, the brotherhood attempts to take it from them and leave the Citadel. Such an outcome could effectively end the adventure, so the encounter must be judged very carefully.

Down the hallway, you hear shouts and angry intonations. Suddenly, a group of people turns the corner. They are engaged in deep conversation and are pushing one another into the wall. Above them floats a magical light.

"I still believe that the primordial order of all things begins with ooze," says one of the men. He is a gigantic blob of a person. He wears a stained and greasy night shirt, has long gray hair down the middle of his back, and gigantic bags droop under his fleshy eyes.

"What are you talking about, Sludgebearer?" a woman responds. "You just said *order*. What do you know about the purity of the ooze if you used the word *order* in the same breath?" She pushes the obese blob into a wall, making a loud slap of flesh against stone. Her long dark hair has not seen a comb in at least a decade, and her skin looks rotted. She wears a simple purple tunic that is badly in need of repair. Without warning, the woman begins to retch and looks as if she will be sick.

"Shut up, Slimetalker," speaks the group's tallest member. "You are obviously still addled — the truth of chaos is embodied within the ever-changing perfection of slime." The man wears a heavy brown robe. He has a vulture-like neck and an enormous mole at the end of the crooked nose. Leaning on a twisted piece of black wood as he walks, the man seems to be sweating profusely.

"Quagmire, if I may say something," asks a similarly robed man. This member of the group has no hair at all, and his skin is heavily wrinkled and covered in thick, viscous goo.

"No, you may not," Quagmire says, taking a slow jab at the smaller man with his staff. The other man jumps out of the way, which causes the final member of their group trip over him.

Jumping to her feet, the thick and squat woman with short-cropped hair points in your general direction. Wearing a nearly transparent pink robe that reveals, among other things, boils all over her body, the woman seems otherwise unarmed. She shouts, "Look!"

The entire group falls silent, staring at you with narrowing eyes.

The Brotherhood of the Ooze is led by Quagmire, a **cult fanatic** with the following changes:

- He has 55 (10d8 + 10) hit points
- He is Challenge Rating of 5 (TBD XP)
- He has Dexterity and Wisdom 16 (+3)
- He has AC 15 (*+1 leather armor*)
- He wields a *staff of sludge* (see **Appendix A**)
- He has a *potion of healing* and a *potion of greater healing*.
- He is a 10th level spellcaster with a spell save DC 14 and +6 to hit with spell attacks
- His prepared spells are:
  · Cantrips (at will): *guidance*, *light*, *resistance*, *sacred flame*, *thaumaturgy*
  · 1st level (4 slots): *bane*, *command*, *cure wounds*, *green water* (see **Appendix A**), *inflict wounds*
  · 2nd level (3 slots): *blindness/deafness*, *hold person*, *silence*
  · 3rd level (3 slots): *bestow curse*, *mass healing word*, *muck* (see **Appendix A**)
  · 4th level (3 slots): *freedom of movement*, *mucus mask* (see **Appendix A**)
  · 5th level (2 slots): *insect plague*, *slime bucket* (see **Appendix A**)

Quagmire carries 10 gems (each worth 1d4 x 100 gp).

Description: Quagmire is a tall and lanky man. He has an enormous mole on the end of a crooked nose, and tufts of bristly brown hair sprout sporadically around his egg-shaped head. Quagmire wears the long thick brown robes of his order and leans on the twisted *staff of sludge* (see **Appendix A**). His appearance is not nearly as nasty as his horrific personality — for he is sadistic and self-loathing. Quagmire is the quintessential grumpy leader.

Background: Quagmire — even he doesn't remember his original name — was once a sculptor. For years he tried to create a perfect sculpture of a paramour. Although his skills were strong, he was never satisfied with his results. Eventually, he made a pact with the Faceless Lord to give him the ability to accomplish this task. In exchange for the ability, Quagmire devoted his soul to the demon. The Faceless Lord turned the sculptor's beloved into stone and tricked Quagmire into believing that he had accomplished the task. When Quagmire discovered his folly, he grew mad with rage and lost his sanity. Now, many years later, his hatred of his master has spurred Quagmire to devote himself faithfully to the Faceless Lord in the hope that the Faceless Lord will destroy him and allow him the death for which he yearns. Unfortunately, the Faceless Lord finds the tormented life of Quagmire humorous and amusing.

Motivation: Quagmire is the leader of the brotherhood because he has served the Faceless Lord the longest and can yell the loudest. He believes that the Faceless Lord has sent the brotherhood on a suicide mission to retrieve the key. He relishes the opportunity to meet his end; however, he will not act foolishly.

Another member of the brotherhood is the massively obese Sludgebearer, a **slime mendicant** (see **Appendix B**). He carries a *potion of greater healing*.

Description: Sludgebearer is a disgusting blob of a person. Looks are deceiving, though, as he can use the morass of slime about him to move with amazing speed. Instead of the long brown robes of his brothers, he wears a greasy nightshirt and cap. Sludgebearer also has long, greasy gray hair and sunken eyes. He rarely speaks.

Background: Once a good-aligned monk, Sludgebearer now barely remembers his name and the name of the deity to whom he was devoted. Sludgebearer long ago committed a grave sin that turned him from the light. Finding solace in food, he quickly became a glutton. Quagmire found him in this state and recruited him for the brotherhood.

Motivation: Sludgebearer cares not for his fellow brothers. He simply desires to kill as a means of striking out at a world that turned its back on him. Sludgebearer has a deep-seated hate for Quagmire due to his years serving with him.

The third member of the Brotherhood of the Ooze is the not entirely sane Slimetalker, a **mage** with the following changes:

- She has AC 13 (*ring of protection*) or 16 (*ring of protection* with *mage armor*).
- She has the following action:
  · **Purity of Slime (1/day).** Slimetalker summons a **gelatinous cube** that appears in an unoccupied space that she can see within 40 feet. The summoned cube is friendly to Slimetalker and her companions. Roll initiative for the gelatinous cube, which has its own turns. The cube disappears after 10 minutes.
- She has a jug of *liquor of vomit* (see **Appendix A**).
- She has a *spell scroll* of *rot to the core* (see **Appendix A**).
- Her prepared spells are:
  · Cantrips (at will): *acid splash*, *minor illusion*, *poison spray*, *true strike*
  · 1st level (4 slots): *charm person*, *mage armor*, *magic missile*, *shield*
  · 2nd level (3 slots): *acid arrow*, *blur*, *invisibility*,
  · 3rd level (3 slots): *counterspell*, *ooze bolt* (see **Appendix A**),
  · 4th level (3 slots): *mucus mask* (see **Appendix A**), *slimeball* (see **Appendix A**)
  · 5th level (1 slot): *cloudkill*

Slimetalker carries 12 gems (each worth 1d4 x 100 gp).

Description: Slimetalker is short and fair, with long dark hair in knots and tangles. She wears a simple purple tunic showing off her bruised and torn skin. She always expresses an opinion but follows whoever is in charge of the brotherhood.

Background: Slimetalker is a former spy for the church of a Lawful deity. She was charged with infiltrating the brotherhood and determining the level of threat it posed. Unfortunately, her ruse was discovered, and she was forced to drink a strange sludge concoction: the *liquor of vomit* (see **Appendix A**). The drink made her thoroughly evil, and to this day she is prone to vomit at inopportune times as a result of imbibing the potion.

Motivation: Slimetalker speaks in between belches. She willingly serves the brotherhood as a mindless zealot.

The next Brother of the Ooze is Muckcreeper, a bloodthirsty **killer** (see **Appendix B**) with the following changes:

- He has 43 (8d8 + 8) hit points.
- He has a *shortsword of venom* (functions exactly as a *dagger of venom* with shortsword damage) instead of an ordinary shortsword.
- He has a *potion of greater healing* a *potion of invisibility*, and a *potion of poison*

Muckcreeper carries 12 gems (each worth 1d4 x 100 gp).

Description: Muckcreeper is short, and his face is heavily scarred from acid. Like Quagmire, he wears the robes of the brotherhood. He has no hair at all. His skin is heavily wrinkled from prolonged exposure to the prismatic slime that seeps from his skin. Muckcreeper is talkative but prefers talking to his sword above anyone else.

Background: Muckcreeper was a street urchin whom Quagmire took as a slave. Muckcreeper grew to hate Quagmire. Still, he took his licks and learned to appreciate the chaos that the brotherhood seeds throughout the world.

Motivation: Muckcreeper believes that he is almost ready to lead. Unlike Quagmire, he is fully devoted to the utter chaos that the Faceless Lord represents. Thus, Muckcreeper is biding his time before he takes over the brotherhood. He truly puts his heart into his work and revels in the blood of his victims. Muckcreeper is the most likely to run and escape from an encounter with the characters.

Last, and perhaps least, in the brotherhood is Oozespouter a **slime initiate** (see **Appendix B**). She has a *potion of flying* and 4 gems (each worth 1d4 x 100 gp).

Description: Oozespouter is a thick and squat woman. She has extremely short-cropped brown hair, and boils are everywhere on her skin. She wears a bright pink robe that is torn. She is prone to breaking down and bawling during combat.

Background: Oozespouter was stolen from an orphanage by Quagmire when she was a very young girl. Living the life of a virtual slave, she idolized Quagmire and emulated every aspect of him. She is also completely infatuated with Sludgebearer, who has been reluctantly showing her the ways of the monk.

Motivation: Oozespouter deeply desires to be accepted. She always tried to find this acceptance from Quagmire; later, she tried to find what she desires from Sludgebearer. Although Sludgebearer has taught her some of his skills, Oozespouter still yearns for guidance. Of the brotherhood, she is the most likely to help the characters.

Oozespouter surrenders to the characters if battle is hopeless for the brotherhood. She bows down and begs for mercy immediately. This act enrages the other members of the brotherhood and they attack her.

Once in a situation where Oozespouter is on speaking terms with the characters (as opposed to at the business end of a weapon), she attempts to escape at the earliest possible opportunity. If the characters make a bargain with her, however, she keeps the bargain. Oozespouter prizes her life and is highly motivated by evenhanded promises to spare her life in exchange for cooperation. Dark threats only encourage her to run during the next battle in which the characters participate.

Tactics: The characters likely catch the brotherhood off-guard. The brotherhood is immediately hostile to the characters if they are in the company of the Cabal of the Beard since the brotherhood hates all dwarves for imprisoning their lord. If possible, the brotherhood attempts to learn what the characters are doing before attacking. The brotherhood has no idea what the key is, but makes many inquiries about it. If the brotherhood somehow learns that the key opens the vault, they make a grab for it and attempt a mad dash for the exit.

THE SILVER EYES

The Silver Eyes were originally a group of drow who came to the surface seeking their lot among the "weaker species." Running afoul of their patron demoness, they left the Under Realms in the service of a new patron — a duke of the hells. At this devil's behest, the Silver Eyes recently "replaced" one of their members with another Under Realms' outcast: an encephalon gorger. Although the devil rarely calls upon their service, he has sent many visions to them ordering the retrieval of the Faceless Lord's amulet.

The Silver Eyes are a methodical and calculating bunch of rogues. They do not attack unless confident that their plan will work. In other words, the Silver Eyes constantly monitor the situation with *clairvoyance* and other means of scrying before attacking.

The bone devil spy (see **Chapter Three**) is an advanced scout for the Silver Eyes. His report (or lack thereof) spurs the group into action. This group could be placed in either the "Siege of Orcus" or "Necromantic Dreams."

Mandan Silvereyes, the leader of the group, is a **bandit captain** with the following changes:

- She has the innate spellcasting and racial characteristics of a **drow.**
- She also speaks Elvish and Undercommon.

- She has the following new ability:
  - **Sneak Attack.** Once per turn, Mandan can deal an extra 10 (3d6) damage to one creature she hits with an attack if she has advantage on the attack roll. She must use a finesse or ranged weapon. Mandan doesn't need advantage on the attack roll if another enemy of the target is within 5 feet of it, that enemy isn't incapacitated, and Mandan doesn't have disadvantage on the attack roll.
- She has the skill Sleight of Hand +4
- She has AC 16 (*+1 studded leather*)
- She has a *javelin of lightning*, a *+1 warhammer*, a *potion of greater healing*, a *potion of invisibility*, 285 gp, and 7 gems (each worth 1d4 x 100 gp).

Description: Mandan Silvereyes is a gorgeous drow elf with flowing white hair and flashing silver eyes. She is as deadly as she is beautiful, however. She wears studded leather armor etched with drow figures performing unspeakable acts. Mandan carries a large, crude hammer, a boon from a battle with deep gnomes.

Background: Mandan Silvereyes began life as a scion of a powerful drow household. Yet like many drow scions, her house was destroyed before she could assassinate her way to power. She lays the blame for this event at the feet of the Queen of Spiders. Thus, she has no time for spiders. Finding other "orphans" of a similar mind, she led them to the surface and rules them through wit and will. Jurak threatens her position, however, because of guidance from the devil they serve.

Motivation: Greed, lust, and self-preservation motivate Mandan Silvereyes. She may change goals on a whim. She will, though, plan any confrontation thoroughly. She cares little about the other members of her group and sees them only as pawns to help her accomplish her goals.

Another of the Silver Eyes band is Epar Griz, an **assassin** with the following changes:

- He has the innate spellcasting and racial characteristics of a **drow**.
- He has Dexterity 20 (+5)
- He also speaks Elvish and Undercommon.
- He wears *boots of haste* (see **Appendix A**).
- He has AC 17 (*cloak of greater protection*, see **Appendix A**).

Epar Griz carries 83 gp and 5 gems (each worth 1d6 x 100 gp).

Description: Epar Griz is boastful and arrogant. He wears a black scarf on his head and occasionally spits between a huge gap in his front teeth. Epar never sits still and has a tendency to talk rapidly (spraying spit all over whomever he is talking to). Epar Griz wears no armor because he is amazingly quick.

Background: Epar Griz tells whoever will listen that he is a bastard child of a high priestess. The truth is that his boasting is a veil for the fact that he is actually a drow of low birth. Also, despite his arrogance, he is actually a very good thief.

Motivation: Like Mandan, Epar Griz is motivated by coin. The adventure and constant danger he and his companions experience excites him. Epar is wary of the recent addition of the encephalon gorger and absolutely hates the worship of the devil — to whom he is only paying lip service for the time being.

Another influential member of the Silver Eyes is Jurak Grubber, a **priest of Orcus** (see **Appendix B**) with the following changes:

- She has the innate spellcasting and racial characteristics of a **drow.**
- She also speaks Elvish and Undercommon.
- She has AC 19 (chainmail, *+1 shield*)

Description: Jurak Grubber is an attractive drow who shaved off all her hair, leaving only a topknot. She frequently uses white makeup to create a skull visage on her face. Jurak communicates with the devil who sent them on the mission to retrieve the amulet from the characters; however, she receives her powers from her true master, Orcus. Although younger than the other drow, her fervor and devotion to Orcus gained her an ally in Sinad.

Background: Jurak, like Mandan, was a progeny of a noble drow house. Yet unlike Mandan, her house was not destroyed. Instead, Jurak willingly left to discover more of the Lord of Undead after learning of him from a visiting encephalon gorger dignitary. Jurak wants to lead the group back into the Under Realms, as she has megalomaniacal dreams of converting all drow to Orcus.

Motivation: Jurak is a megalomaniac; she believes that Orcus has made her nearly invincible. She views Mandan with disdain but sees her as a tolerable nuisance until she gains enough of Orcus' favor to lead an army of undead to convert the drow populace. She is excited that the encephalon gorger joined them because it tilted the scales in the group in her favor over Mandan. She feels great distaste in working with the devil, but she plots to take the amulet for Orcus.

Filling out the ranks of the group, Sinad is a drow **mage** with the following changes:

- He has the innate spellcasting and racial characteristics of a **drow**,
- He is a 12th level spellcaster with spell save DC 15, and +6 to hit with spell attacks.
- His higher level prepared spells are:
  5th level (2 slots): *cone of cold, dominate person*
  6th level (1 slot): *disintegrate*
- He has 54 (12d8) hit points
- He has AC 14 (*bracers of defense*) or 17 (*bracers of defense* and *mage armor*)
- He has a *wand of magic missiles*.
- He has a *figurine of wondrous power (onyx dog)*

Description: Sinad is a morose drow who left the Under Realms to learn more of the surface world. He is quiet and rarely speaks. When he does speak, however, Mandan usually considers his words. Sinad is secretly in love with Jurak. He wears a long drow robe of bluish hue and has a large mane of white hair and piercing violet eyes.

Background: Sinad's parents ordered his death when he refused to yield his position as a high wizard to lead his family's estate. Eventually, he dealt with his parents by devastating the household and killing many of its servants. These acts made him an outcast, and Mandan eventually recruited him.

Motivation: Sinad is quiet and calculating, but he has the potential for great destruction (as his parents discovered). Sinad bears a deep affection for Jurak. Although he usually sides with her, his intellect does not allow him to let emotions rule his mind. He is curious about the encephalon gorger and sometimes engages it in hours of metaphysical discussion.

Finally, the most recent addition to the Silver Eyes, Bleela, is an **encephalon gorger** (see **Appendix B**)

Description: Bleela is a typical encephalon gorger. She (it refers to itself as she) wears long purple and pink robes, a square hat, and many jewels and gold trinkets.

Background: Bleela was ordered to serve a visiting priest of Orcus as part of an evil pact between the church of Orcus and the encephalon gorgers. The priest in turn gave Bleela's service to Jurak (immediately before Jurak murdered the priest). Bleela then disposed of the previous party member, whom Jurak did not like. She is very much a cold and calculating killer.

Motivation: Bleela thinks not of herself. She has devoted herself in undertaking the boon to the servants of Orcus until such time that the service is at an end. At that time, Bleela simply feeds on the minds of her companions and returns to her former life.

IMBO THE UNDYING

Born to a whore — this is how **Imbo the Undying** (see **Appendix B**) began life in the cruel world. Reminded of his parentage and the limitless possibilities of his father, the young dwarf was beaten and brutalized throughout his childhood. Eventually running away from his broken home, Imbo was captured by a group of barbarian raiders.

Unaware of Imbo's past, the barbarians treated Imbo the same as they treated all of their children — that is, poorly. The barbarians trained Imbo to track, to hunt, and to wield a warhammer. Imbo learned his lessons well but was ever the outsider, not being human born.

In adolescence, Imbo began to covet wealth. When booty was available, Imbo frequently held back a shiny object or item. Later, he began to steal items. Although there were whispers and a few open accusations, nothing done to the dwarf. Late one night, Imbo tried to steal the warband leader's golden horn. The chieftain caught Imbo in this treacherous act, and Imbo slew his foster father in a fit of rage. He then fled into the night.

Many years later, Imbo was an accomplished thief. He found his way into a village of elves. After an elf insulted his parentage (although the elf had no idea of the truth of it), Imbo went on a bloody spree. Within hours, the entire village was either dead or had fled into the wilderness.

The final victim for Imbo's cruelty was an ancient and withered elf, but she did not beg for mercy. Before dying, she told Imbo, "For the blackness of your heart and the sins you commit, you shall be ever reminded and know no rest."

Imbo learned later the actual effect of the curse: He could not die. He could be subdued, disintegrated, or even, on one occasion, consumed; however, his life would always, eventually come back. His anger at this prospect grew greater as the years wore on.

Now fully consumed by hatred, Imbo has become wrath incarnate. Thoroughly evil, Imbo does not hesitate to commit the foulest acts that his perverse mind can concoct. Menacing and brooding, Imbo does not hesitate to rain his ever-burning hatred upon those around him to occupy the emptiness in his soul that the fates have spun for him.

Particularly wealthy and evil individuals frequently hire Imbo as a mercenary. An astute warrior, a remarkable thief, and an evil force unto himself, Imbo is without remorse, without fear, and he brings carnage wherever he roams.

RAOB AND SLEEARA

Another set of NPCs could be Raob and Sleeara. Raob has the statistics of a **commander** (see **Appendix B**) with the following changes:

- He wields a *+2 flail* with which he is +9 to hit and does 10 (1d8 + 6) bludgeoning damage).
- He has AC 21 (*+1 plate armor*, shield)

Sleeara has the statistics of a **death mage** (see **Appendix B**) with the following changes:

- She has a *staff of power*.
- She has AC 18 (*robe of the archmagi* and *ring of protection*)
- She has a spell save DC 17 and a +9 to spell attacks due to her robe
- Her Challenge Rating is 11 (7,200 XP)

Placing these two with a number of Raob's sergeants would be an easy way for you to deal with characters needing to eliminate Raob and his army completely if they leave the Citadel. The sergeants use the statistics of a **guard** with the following changes:

- They have 39 [6d8 + 12] hit points
- They have a longsword attack (+4 to hit, 6 [1d8 + 2] slashing damage)
- They have a longbow attack (+4 to hit, 6 [1d8 + 2] piercing damage)
- Their Challenge Rating is 1 (200 XP)

Each guard carries 1d4 gems (each worth 1d10 x 10 gp).

Basically, any dead guards or any sign of disturbance shows Sleeara that someone entered the Citadel. She already knows that the army has been digging directly into the granite and not finding any artifacts, bodies, or even rooms. She already suspects something. With her knowledge of arcana, the Devil's Finger, and dwarven magic, she and Raob could travel back in time and into the Citadel in either the "Siege of Orcus" or "Necromantic Dreams."

DWURSCHMIEDE: THE CITADEL

The following areas of the Citadel are briefly described. They are depicted on **Map B: Upper Halls** and **Map C: Lower Halls** The appropriate sets of encounters are left for you to insert, depending on which era the characters are currently investigating (either the "Siege of Orcus" or "Necromantic Dreams"). This is an excellent opportunity to challenge fully but not overwhelm the characters by scaling the encounters up or down where appropriate.

AREA B-1: THE GRAND HALL

A long hallway lies before the characters. Colorful banners hang from a 20-foot-high ceiling and depict horns, a helm, an axe, and similar symbols. As well, a large red and black banner proclaims these halls as the abode of Clan Flammeaxte. The granite has changed from the rough grayish rock as it appears outside on the surface of the Devil's Finger. Here, the granite is a polished red. Arches carved in the ceiling proclaim in an ancient Dwarven dialect, "Welcome Friend!" and "Death to Fiend!" Small, five-foot-wide-by-five-foot-tall hallways lead off on both sides.

AREA B-2: THE STAIRS

Hanging from a 20-foot-high ceiling is an elaborate black, wrought-iron candelabra. On opposite walls, two sets of polished stairs lead down. To the north, the corridor splits left and right. Lining the walls to the north are polished skulls of orcs, elves, and other humanoids. Mixed among them are strange black skills with spiraling horns and large fanged teeth.

The candelabra is raised and lowered by a chain in the northwest corner. A stone bench is in the corner for the guards. A dwarf-hair blanket is underneath the bench. The dwarves of the Citadel in times of shame cut off their beards, and their wives and loved ones routinely take the hair and make it into something useful as a symbol of redemption.

The stairs here are trapped. In each staircase is a random stair an inch or two shorter than the rest. An examination and a successful DC 12 Intelligence (Investigation) check discovers the trap. Each character that steps on the altered step without being aware of its nature must succeed on a DC 12 Dexterity check or trip and take 3 (1d6) bludgeoning damage. This rudimentary trap is to trip invaders who are unfamiliar with the stairs. The characters will likely encounter someone in this heavily trafficked area; roll for the possibility of a random encounter in either time period.

AREA B-3: WORKSHOP

Wooden benches and tables line the perimeter of this room. A large brazier sits in the center. On the wall are wooden pegs with aprons hanging from them. Runes written along the ceiling at odd intervals proclaim the greatness of Dwurfater and ask for his blessing in the crafting below.

AREA B-4: STORAGE

This room has numerous stone shelves full of metal boxes and foodstuffs. The dwarves use this room to store food and basic supplies (bandages, empty flasks, dried meats, and so forth). In a corner is a broken wooden spoon where a particularly greedy dwarf was eating the stores. Bundles of twine are also lying about. Other than these ordinary items, there is nothing special about these rooms.

AREA B-5: BARRACKS

Rows of triple bunk beds line this room; the beds are made of stained wood. Weapons and armor are ready for use in racks lining the wall. A few footlockers are set near the beds. Several piles of stones — chits from gambling games played by the dwarves — are in the corner of one of the barracks. A small kobold drum made of human skin and bone that has "Gog" written on it is in another.

AREA B-6: KITCHEN

Various iron pots hang from the low ceiling of this room. A shelf carved in the wall has numerous tins for dwarven spices, and painted on the tins are such names as "shale oil," "mountain mint," and "sprig of toadstool." The spice rack has a recipe for Kobold Kidney Pie carved into it. Large black pots sit on stoves cut into the floor. Small, three-inch-wide chimneys carry the smoke from the stoves into the Finger. The entire area is very cramped and crowded.

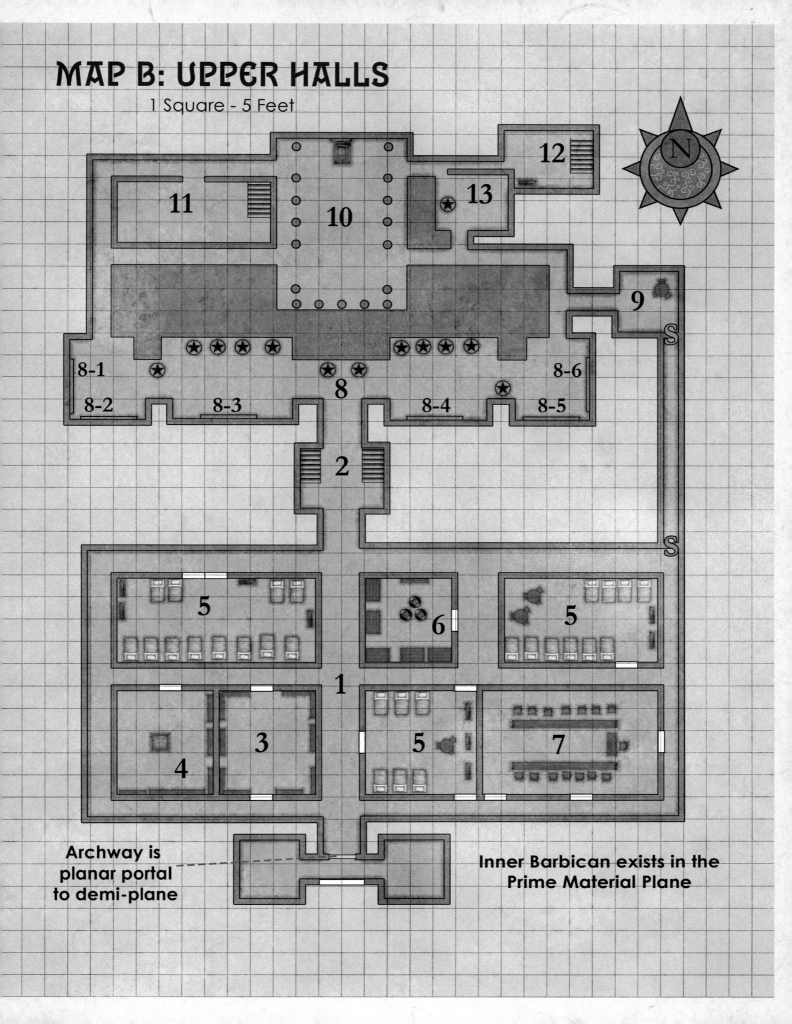

MAP B: UPPER HALLS

1 Square - 5 Feet

N

S

S

11

10

12

13

9

8-1

8-2

8-3

8

8-4

8-5

8-6

2

5

6

5

1

3

4

5

7

Archway is
planar portal
to demi-plane

Inner Barbican exists in the
Prime Material Plane

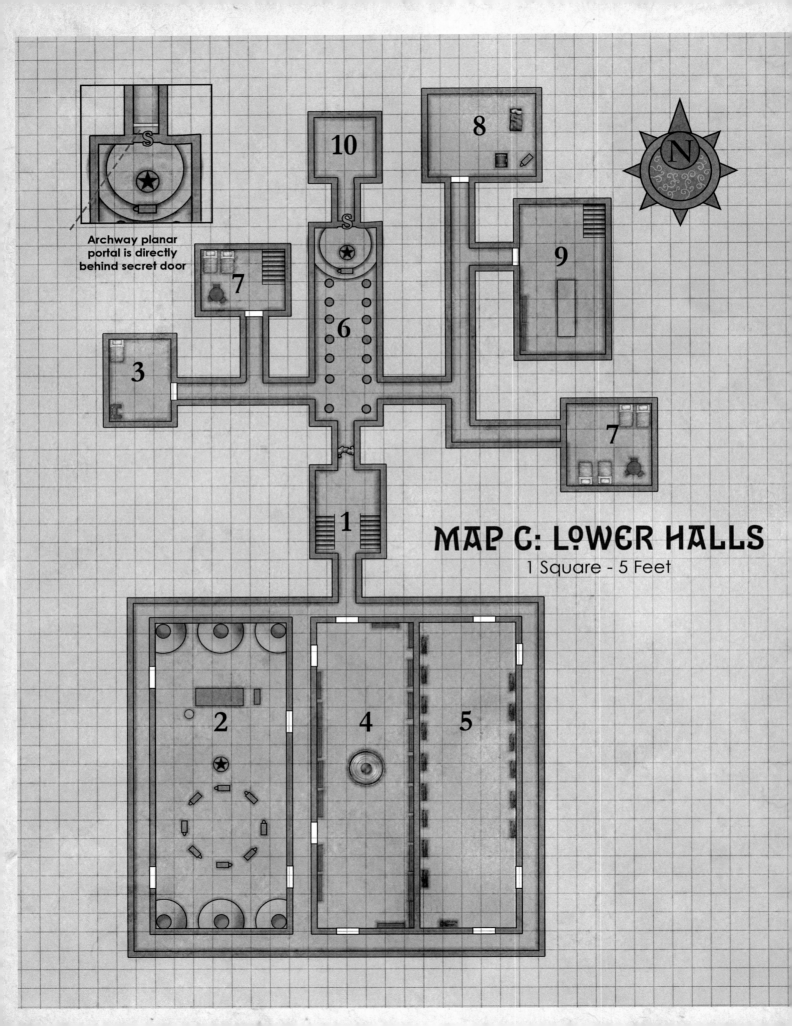

Archway planar portal is directly behind secret door

S

10

8

S

7

6

9

3

7

1

MAP C: LOWER HALLS
1 Square - 5 Feet

2

4

5

N

Area B-7: Mess Hall

Long wooden tables and chairs form a square in this room. Shields with dwarven heraldry are set on the walls. A large chair — the only chair in the room — sits at one end of the square. Numerous brass steins hang on one wall, and a forgotten brass tapper lies underneath a bench. At each place on the tables are placed a small wooden spoon, a sharp knife, and a wooden plate.

Area B-8: Hall of Heroes

Numerous carvings and statues line the length of this hall from west to east. All the statues depict menacing, snarling dwarves with large axes. The carvings show the Citadel's history.

The first carving depicts a mountain and a great cube falling from the sky. The mountain breaks apart in the next pane, with a dwarf in the corner covering his head with an arm. The third pane shows the Devil's Finger where the mountain once stood with the cube on its top.

The second carving shows dwarves climbing to the top of the Citadel. The second pane shows an upside-down crescent with spikes protruding from it in all directions within the cube and the dwarves kneeling and worshipping it. Very observant individuals notice tiny eyes with flecks of ruby all over the stone carving. The shards are worthless. The third pane shows a great dwarf god looking over a cloud high above the Citadel with a look of disbelief on his face.

The third carving shows the great dwarf god pointing at his worshippers. The next pane shows row after row of dwarven smiths hammering on a gigantic anvil. The final pane displays a circle of dwarves surrounding the anvil beneath the Devil's Finger.

The fourth carving depicts the anvil sitting atop the cube. A rising moon in the distance is smeared with a brown paint that looks like dried blood. The next pane shows a column of swirling liquid with many eyes. In the final pane, the dwarf god smiles above the crescent. Spikes are on top of the anvil, which sits on top of the cube, which rests on top of the swirling column.

The fifth carving shows the dwarf god looking down from a cloud high above the Devil's Finger, pointing at the cube. The next two panes show construction of the Citadel's towers and barbican.

The sixth carving is visible in "Necromantic Dreams" but not in the "Siege of Orcus." It shows demons invading the halls of the Citadel. If the characters assisted the dwarves in defeating the demons, it shows the faces and bodies of the characters and describes in two panes the events that transpired earlier. Alternately, it could show the characters decimating the dwarves or the dwarves driving them back and defeating them.

Area B-9: Guard Room

This side guard room is the station area for the lord of the Citadel's personal guards. The guards use the secret passage only in emergencies to escape or to flank any assault in the stair area. The room has a small round table with chairs. The table has many notches, the result of the guards keeping score while playing dice or other games. A cracked ivory pipe is on the table.

Area B-10: Great Hall

This is the grand reception hall of the Citadel's lord. Great columns are carved from the same stone as the ceiling and the floor. These columns are ornately decorated with Dwarvish runes that list the many dwarves who died creating the Citadel. On the far end is a great throne on a dais that rises five feet above the floor. Both throne and dais are carved directly out of the granite. The throne is in the shape of an anvil with a depression in it for the lord of the Citadel to sit. The ceiling of the room is 40 feet high. This room is directly beneath the vault.

Area B-11: Guest Quarters

This is one of the most elaborately furnished rooms in the Citadel. It has an unusual bed of elaborate craftsmanship. The wooden bed is canopied and can be adjusted in length or width to fit any creature from three to seven feet tall. A large painting on one wall depicts dwarves fighting elves. The scene in the painting, however, changes as one moves by it. From one angle, it shows the battle; from another angle, it shows the elves and dwarves embracing as brothers. It is magical and was a gift from an elf diplomat. (See **Appendix A** for more information on the *painting of enlightenment*.)

The room also contains chairs, a dressing table, and a rack for weapons and armor. A large ogre skin rug lies on the floor. The ogre's skull is on display near the stairs (**Area B-2**).

Area B-12: Galm's Quarters

The lord of the Citadel during the "Siege of Orcus" is King Galm. His spartan lifestyle removed all frivolity from the room. There is a simple, hard bed, a rack for his battleaxe, and a stand for his elaborate armor. A footstool hidden underneath the bed has an elf's face on it. Galm said that he would use the stool to talk eye-to-eye with elves, but demanded that he be allowed to step on an elf's face to do so.

Area B-13: Reception Area

A map of the surrounding countryside is inlaid on the floor in this room. The only furniture is a large throne for the Citadel's lord, who comes here in order to make plans to repel sieges. A large ruby is set in the center of the map. Anyone saying "map" in an ancient Dwarvish dialect activates an illusion showing the Devil's Finger and the surrounding countryside. This is the only means by which the dwarves kept track of the immediate outside world. Although traveling to the outside world was forbidden, there were times when the dwarves made small excursions. The ruby can be removed with a successful DC 15 Dexterity check with thieves' tools. A failed check destroys the stone. The ruby does not function if removed and is worth 5,000 gp.

Area C-1: Stairs Below

This area is identical to the stairs on the upper level (**Area B-2**). This stair, however, had a trap that was triggered with the arrival of the demons in the "Siege of Orcus." The trap released large boulders and rubble to block the south passageway.

Area C-2: Forge

This large area is the Citadel's central smithing facility. Numerous forges, bellows, and elaborate chimneys line the walls. The chimneys are made of metal and take the heat and smoke off at angles; they enter the walls and funnel the smoke and fires to the side of the Citadel. The very-narrow chimneys cannot be traversed by any non-magical means. In the center of the room are a number of anvils that form a circle around a small statue of Dwurfater that shows the god with a sour expression on his face, as if he is never satisfied with the smiths.

Area C-3: Kinst's Chambers

This is the bedchambers of Kinst, the traitor. Kinst has very gaudy taste for a dwarf. A number of chalk drawings on the wall show the Devil's Finger from various angles. Each drawing is signed with a gigantic Dwarvish "K." The drawings emphasize the vault, making it appear larger than it is in reality. Kinst's bed is a simple cot, but he has an elaborately carved dresser and the only mirror in the entire Citadel.

The wall-mounted mirror is magical and allows Kinst to communicate with others outside the Citadel. The mirror functions exactly like a *crystal ball of telepathy*. Orcus plotted with Kinst concerning the Citadel's demise through this mirror. If removed from the wall, the mirror loses its magical properties.

Area C-4: Armory

Rack after rack of weapons and armor stand ready to be used against any aggressors who attack the Citadel. You must decide what the characters find here. A few of the weapons are magical, but most of those weapons are already in the possession of the dwarves encountered in the "Siege of Orcus" due to the preparations for the demon invasion.

Area C-5: Storage

This massive storage area holds food and drinking water. A font in the middle of the room magically provides spring water; the water is drinkable in either dimension. The foodstuffs are either pungent dwarven cheeses, hearty ales, disgusting brandy, hard breads, and dried meats in the "Siege of Orcus," or dust on empty shelves in "Necromantic Dreams."

AREA C-6: TEMPLE OF DWURFATER

This room has a high ceiling with columns identical to the Great Hall (**Area C-11**). At the far end is an altar upon which rests a large statue of Dwurfater readying a great blow with his hammer on a large anvil. Behind Dwurfater is a secret door; any hammer obtained from **Area C-4** will open the secret door if struck upon the anvil. The hammer in Dwurfater's hand is part of the stone block from which the statute was carved. Breaking the hammer from the statute and using it to hit the anvil does nothing. The anvil shows many depressions from a hammer striking it. Below the anvil is an inscription in an ancient dialect of Dwarvish that reads: "With a Dwarven Blow, I Protect My Children."

This is the only way to open the magical door, as it was created by arcane dwarven magics.

AREA C-7: PRIEST QUARTERS

This is the quarters of the priests attending to Usis, the high priest of Dwurfater. This room has a number of beds and tables. Many holy symbols are carved into the ceiling, arranged in a circle and depicting the dwarven pantheon with Dwurfater's anvil large in the center.

AREA C-8: USIS' QUARTERS

Usis, high priest of Dwurfater, made his home here. During the "Siege of Orcus," he fell very ill and is comatose with priests attending him. This was the work of Kinst. The room has a simple cot, a small anvil shrine to Dwurfater, and an unlocked chest full of vestments and robes.

AREA C-9: BURIAL PREPARATION AND MASONRY

Most dwarves are burned in the great forges when they die. For the kings, their tenure as guardians remains in the afterlife. The priests use this room to prepare these bodies after death for burial in the catacombs below. The dwarves are not experts in mummification, but they do use oils and spices to prepare the body; a long stone slab is used for this purpose. Funerary oils and spices that smell very caustic are on a shelf.

The other part of the room is a storage area for mining tools (picks, shovels, and carts). These are sacramental tools used by the new dwarven king to bury the recently deceased lord. The mining tools are always caked with stone dust, for cleaning them is sacrilege, and they are usually lying about haphazardly.

AREA C-10: LOWER ARCHWAY

Hidden behind the statue of Dwurfater (**Area C-6**) is the lower archway, which is identical to the upper archway. This lower archway is accessible only with the rune belonging to the dwarven king, without which anyone entering the archway is lost through time. It is visible only from the stairwell side. Looking back through the archway, the characters see most of the temple collapsed due to the temporal anchors protecting the archway. Entering the archway from the catacomb side sends the characters into "Necromantic Dreams."

The stairwell is a gigantic spiral staircase. The center is open, and the end of the stairs is 75 feet below.

CHAPTER THREE:
DESCENT –
THE SIEGE OF ORCUS

The characters enter the Citadel's demiplane through the upper archway. At the same time, the characters travel back 3,000 years and arrive during a siege by the minions of Orcus. A traitor to the dwarves is about to open a portal. Orcus wants to overrun the dwarves and take the Faceless Lord's amulet for himself and add to his own power.

The specific encounters described herein pertain to a portal that opens moments after the characters arrive. Orcus conspired with a cowardly dwarf priest named Kinst. With the dwarf's assistance, Orcus pierced the Citadel's magical wards to open the portal.

Orcus provided Kinst with the means to create an evil totem that activates the portal. The only way to destroy the portal is to destroy the totem. In other words, the portal functions as per the spell of the same name, except it is permanent and cannot be dispelled but for destroying the totem. This may be difficult for the characters to discern without speaking to Kinst or healing High Priest Usis.

The characters may also befriend the dwarves, which is most likely through the gregarious and charismatic King Galm. Galm is as frightened as any dwarf at first seeing the strange party (unless the party is all dwarves), but he accepts any reasonable explanation if the party is willing to address the current situation. Dwarves are watchful that an invasion is about to occur. The characters must talk quickly to convince the dwarves that they are friends and not foes, as described in **Encounter III-A**.

The demons do not see the party as an ally except in the most unlikely of circumstances. They are intent upon finding the key and taking it as soon as possible. The only avenue for the demons to escape is through the portal, and they cannot *gate* in additional reinforcements. Please note that a good party can indeed summon creatures to its aid, as the magical energies that protect the Citadel allow such magics for the Citadel's defense. The prime goal is for the party to gain access to the catacombs where the key is kept.

If the characters have an easy time dealing with the demons, additional NPC parties from **Chapter Two** can enter the fray. In particular, Raob and Sleeara and/or Imbo the Undying are recommended.

The accompanying sidebar contains a recommended timeline of events. This timeline takes the encounters out of the static and into the dynamic. Also, the timeline assumes no character intervention. Moving the monsters and NPCs makes the battle more realistic; in addition, the intensity of the encounters increases as the demons rampage through the Citadel.

INTRODUCTORY CHARACTERISTICS

Wandering Monsters: The entire Citadel is about to break out into chaos when the characters arrive. They might find the demons attempting to locate the lower archway, though they will more likely run into dwarves bent on routing the demons from their stronghold. Roll 1d20 every 10 minutes.

1d20	Encounter
1	King Galm (**commander**, see **Appendix B**, as modified in **Encounter III-A**)
2–4	2d8 dwarves (**guards** as modified in **Encounter III-A**)
5	The **bone devil** spy from **Encounter III-D**
6–7	1d6 + 2 **dretches**
8	The 2 **succubi** and the dwarven smiths (**guards** as modified in **Encounter III-C**)
9	A **vrock** fighting 1d8 dwarves (**guards** as modified in **Encounter III-A**)
10	One of the NPC parties from **Chapter Two**
11–20	No Encounter

Shielding: As previously described, using *teleport* or other forms of magic to exit the Citadel is impossible.

Detections: Characters detect strong evil in all rooms south of the stairwell on the lower level due to the presence of the *gate* and the demons.

Standard Features: Unless otherwise noted, all doors are on a central pivot and made of stone. The floor, walls, and ceiling are seamless. The rock is polished smooth and has a mirror-like quality; also, every noise echoes throughout the stone structure. Both of these qualities of the Citadel's environment make sneaking about or hiding very difficult. Characters have disadvantage on Dexterity (Stealth) checks. On the other hand, the echo effect makes it easier for a party to hear what is ahead and around the bend. As well, each room is as tall as wide, except where otherwise noted. Thus, a majority of hallways in the Citadel are only five feet tall. In these cramped areas, Medium creatures taller than a dwarf are considered to be squeezing (cutting their speed in half and giving them disadvantage on attack rolls and Dexterity saving throws). The entire Citadel is lit with heavily smoking torches that burn the characters' eyes in crowded areas.

Maps Used: Map B: The Citadel — The Upper Halls; Map C: The Citadel — The Lower Halls.

TIMELINE OF THE SIEGE OF ORCUS

Time (Minutes)	Event
Two days before the characters arrive	High Priest Usis has a vision of demons invading the Citadel.
One day before the characters arrive	Kinst poisons Usis.
00:00	The characters arrive. Kinst murders two dwarves in the armory.
+ 10:00	Kinst opens the gate. Immediately, dretches arrive and begin wandering the Citadel. Various demons enter and begin attacking the dwarves on all levels.
+ 12:00	King Galm becomes aware of the invasion. The order is given to seal the southern halls on Level Two. King Galm desires to fight, but his advisors restrain him for fear that the *portal rune* to the catacombs might fall into the enemy's hands.
+ 13:00	Gleegog and Tarashix (**Encounter III-E**) arrive to secure the gate.
+ 15:00	The southern rubble trap is sprung (**Encounter III-B**).
+ 20:00	The bone devil (**Encounter III-E**) arrives and stealthily evades the demons guarding the gate. The bone devil makes its way to Kinst's chambers.
+ 24:00	Kainhis, leader of the demonic forces, arrives and heads toward **Encounter III-B**.
+ 27:00	Two succubi arrive to take control of the dwarves in **Encounter III-C**.
+ 38:00	Kainhis finishes devouring the dwarves at **Encounter III-B** and heads upstairs.
+ 44:00	The succubi take their dwarven "friends" and slay all of the healers in the northern halls on Level Two. They are assisted by demon reinforcements.
+ 48:00	Kainhis and other demons assault the Main Hall
+ 61:00	Kainhis kills Galm in his chambers. Demons cover her retreat to Level Two.
+ 70:00	The bone devil, realizing the battle is lost, makes his way back to the gate and leaves.
+ 72:00	All demons but Kainhis attack the remaining dwarves. Kinst begins to inscribe the *portal rune* onto himself.
+ 80:00	Kainhis enters the catacombs. All is lost.

DEFENDERS OF THE CITADEL AND LORD GALM

There are 140 dwarves in the complex. They are guards, priests, cooks, lords, and so forth. The adventure assumes that the party attempts to work with the dwarves, though you decide when and where these dwarves are encountered throughout the complex. Many of them might be sleeping, some might be on guard at the stairwell, others could be cooking, or the majority might be outside defending the battlements. By deciding where to place the dwarves, you can control the difficulty of this level.

On the other hand, if you anticipate that your party is likely to fight it out, most of the dwarves are stout fighters.

King Galm is in the reception area (**Area B-14**) working with his advisors. Ever since Usis' prophecy and seemingly related illness, Galm is preparing for the worst. The Citadel has not suffered a breach in almost 300 years, and one is not about to occur during his watch.

The characters will likely encounter King Galm very quickly. If they convince the dwarves in **Encounter III-A** that they are friends and not foes, the dwarves immediately take the characters to Galm. He is loud, boisterous, and rude. He is a kind dwarf at heart, though, and is the first to believe the characters if they tell the truth of how they arrived at the Citadel. During this conversation, a guard rushes into the room warning of demons below. Galm wants to take care of this evil personally. Yet he is restrained. One of Galm's advisors — or perhaps Galm himself — recommends that the "purportedly good" characters remove the threat while the dwarves attempt to protect Galm and contain the demons that gained access to Level One. If the characters are amenable, this solidifies an alliance with the dwarves and is very likely to lead to Galm giving them the necessary *portal rune* (see **Appendix A**) to enter the catacombs (**Chapter Four**). If the characters bluntly refuse, Galm goes into a tirade and attempts to seize them. Galm is not afraid of any foe.

LOCATION OF DWARVES

A typical distribution of the dwarves when the characters arrive is as follows:

Location	Occupants
Upper Stairs	6 dwarves — guarding the entrance
Workshop	5 dwarves — relentlessly crafting
Barracks	20 dwarves — exhausted from battle and near comatose
Guard Room	6 dwarves — guards
Great Hall	4 dwarves — guards
Reception Area	King Galm and 8 dwarven guards
Lower Stairs	**Encounter III-B**
Forge	**Encounter III-C**
Kinst's Chambers	**Encounter III-D**
Armory	**Encounter III-E**
Temple	2 priests and 10 dwarves
Usis' Chambers	Usis and 4 priests

The comatose Usis is in his quarters, attended by 4 **priests**. Poisoned by Kinst (**Encounter III-D**), Usis is near death. The priests have been able to sustain him but could use the characters help in healing Usis fully. If they help (by casting *greater restoration*, *heal*, *wish*, or a similar spell), he implicates Kinst and demands justice. Usis has received visions in his comatose state from Dwurfater and knows of his folly in trusting Kinst. If the characters are successful, the dwarves reward them with a *+2 warhammer* as a boon from the faithful of Dwurfater (this is Usis' personal weapon). Also, Usis may use the rune on the back of Galm's neck and tattoo the appropriate rune for the characters to move on to the catacombs.

ENCOUNTER III-A: FRIEND OR FOE? (AREA B-1)

As the characters enter the room through the archway on top of the Devil's Finger, they are immediately confronted with 15 dwarves. These are **guards** with a warhammer attack that does 5 (1d8 + 1) bludgeoning damage or 6 (1d10 + 1) bludgeoning damage if wielded with two hands. The dwarves are led by Nukion, a dwarf **knight** with a *+1 longsword* and two *potions of healing*, who is ordered to destroy any demon that enters the upper archway. One of the few dwarves allowed to leave the Dwurschmiede demiplane as a spy in the outside world, Nukion is very suspicious but recognizes the characters as being something other than a demon. Nukion is also the only dwarf who speaks Common. The others can understand Dwarvish, but speak an ancient dialect.

The characters must talk their way out of a direct confrontation. If successful in calming down the frightened and potentially angry dwarves, the characters are immediately escorted to **Area B-14**. Along the way, Nukion is likely to tell them proudly some of the history of Clan Flammeaxte. The king of the dwarves, Galm, is waiting for them. He has the statistics of a **commander** (with a *+2 battleaxe* with which he is +9 to hit and does 10 [1d8 + 6] slashing damage, see **Appendix B**). His crown is a simple band of gold with 3 large rubies worth 2,000 gp each.

Personality: King Galm is very suspicious of any outsiders, but he may view them as a gift of Dwurfater to help the Citadel in its time of greatest need. See **Chapter Two** and above for more information on King Galm's motivations and personality. Galm has the only copy of the necessary *portal rune* (see **Appendix A**) that leads to the catacombs.

If shown the *portal rune* (see **Appendix A**) the characters used to gain access to the Citadel, some of the dwarves might believe that they are celestials sent by Dwurfater to rout the demons. Whether the characters make this belief plausible is to be decided in the events and encounters to come.

ENCOUNTER III-B: THE BARRICADE (AREA C-1)

> Piles of bricks cover the south exit. Twelve dwarves stand with polearms before them pointing at the south pile. A small dwarf woman in a simple white robe grimaces, tears running down her cheek.
> From beyond the south pile comes a muffled scream. Suddenly, the pile shifts and bricks clink together as they are pushed away from the top. Something horrifically foul, smelling of a combination of greasy manure and rotted flesh, is on the other side. The dwarves menacingly grit their teeth. "Stand fast, fellas," one utters.
> At the top of the pile, a hole opens and a gigantic head pops through. With wild yellow eyes, bruise-purple skin, and a gigantic maw, the demon bellows a single word. The dwarves fall aside and break, fleeing in terror, and many fall to the ground in physical pain. The small priestess collapses under the assault, and the demon cackles with delight as it continues to break through the rubble.

The above description should be used if the characters are surprised (likely) by the demon. Although they might prepare themselves, the arrival of a demon combatant can shake any stout soul, causing hesitation.

The **dwarves** — **guards** with a halberd attack that does 6 (1d10 + 1) slashing damage — gathered here to make a stand against the newly arrived demons. By triggering a trap, the dwarves barricaded themselves behind a mass of bricks. The **hezrou** named Kainhis uses its Stench ability to send the dwarves fleeing into the tunnels. The effect poisons Alejan, a **priest** of Dwurfater. Not a warrior, Alejan is shocked by recent events and the arrival of the demon.

Faced with the scattered guards, the characters must now defend the Citadel or quickly move through the northern passage and attempt to find the lower archway. Digging through the northern barrier requires 2d6 rounds of hard work.

Kainhis is the leader of the siege. This is a high honor for her to be granted such a command. Her actions past this room through entering the catacombs are described in the timeline above. Orcus is actually using Kainhis as a vanguard. If Kainhis is successful — and without the characters assisting the dwarves, she very well could be — then Orcus' reliance is well-placed. If Kainhis fails, Orcus sends the guards at the portal (**Encounter III-E**) to acquire the necessary rune.

ENCOUNTER III-C: MOMMY! (AREA C-2)

The heat in the room is oppressive. Numerous twisting metal pipes run along the walls. Smoke fills the air, and flames roar from large forges. In the center of the room are a number of anvils that form a circle around a small statue of a dwarven deity. The deity has a disapproving look on his face as he glares down on the anvils.

No one works at the forges. The dwarven smiths in long aprons sit cross-legged on the floor in the circle around two plump and cherub-faced dwarven women. The women seem to be telling a story of some sort.

The dwarven women speak in soothing tones as they tells the smiths a fable about a little dwarf lost in the great maze of caverns below the surface world. The characters hear part of the tale as they approach, which ends when the lost dwarf's mother finds the little dwarf and escapes the clutches of an evil elf. At the end, both of the dwarven women ask their audience, "Who wants a kiss from mommy?" Two unlucky dwarves eagerly jump up and are smothered by the women.

Unless they intervene, the characters watch in horror as both smiths drop lifelessly to the floor with gigantic grins on their faces. The dwarven women lick their bloody lips and glare at the characters.

The women are 2 **succubi** who have enraptured the group of eight dwarves — as **guards** with a warhammer attack that does 5 (1d8 + 1) bludgeoning damage or 6 (1d10 + 1) bludgeoning damage if wielded with two hands. They ask the characters if they are interested in a kiss. At the same time, the succubi command the dwarves to protect their mommies. The dwarves are happy to oblige and aghast that anyone threatens their mothers.

Tactics: The succubi attempt to use their Charm ability on the characters to convince them to strip off their armor and drop their weapons. If successful, the succubi try to "kiss" the charmed character. Meanwhile, the enraptured dwarves attack, believing that the party members are demons (due to a suggestion by the succubi).

If the party is accompanying a group of dwarves from one of the previous encounters, these dwarves hesitate to attack their brethren. Instead, they try to flank their brothers to get to the succubi.

Eventually, the "mommies" and the dwarves wander the complex and begin wreaking havoc. As a possible wandering encounter, if the succubi have enraptured a large number of dwarven men, then a group of dwarven women wanting to get their men back might join the characters against the succubi.

ENCOUNTER III-D: THE TRAITOR KINST AND THE DEVIL SPY (AREA C-3)

This room is a blast of purple, pink, and orange colors. A number of colorful chalk drawings on the room show the Devil's Finger. There is a simple cot with a bright purple blanket. A large wooden dresser of enameled orange is on one side of the room. A large mirror stands on top of the dresser.

The particularly foul Kinst, a **preacher** (see **Appendix B**) with a *+1 battleaxe* and a *totem of the gate* (see **Appendix A**), hides here while the demons maraud through the lower level. He talks in hushed tones to the the mirror, but the mirror does not respond. The mirror is a magical scrying device that allowed Kinst to communicate with Orcus and plan the assault. Orcus does not answer Kinst now because he has much better things to do. The mirror functions like a *crystal ball of telepathy*. The mirror loses all magical properties if removed from the dresser.

Kinst is a coward, a cheat, and thoroughly evil. The High Priest Usis had a soft spot in his heart for Kinst and believed he could be a great priest dedicated to Dwurfater. Because of this love, Usis was blind to his disciple's treacherous nature.

After Usis predicted the demonic invasion, Kinst poisoned him by coating a manuscript with poison. Usis still has stains from this poison on his fingers. A jar containing one dose of the poison called "demon's ink" is hidden in a locked box under Kinst's cot. The poison is an oil-smelling tar. Anyone opening the jar should must succeed on a DC 10 Dexterity saving throw to avoid initially touching the poison. Anyone failing the save takes 7 (2d6) poison damage.

Kinst used a magical *totem of the gate* (see **Appendix A**) that Orcus instructed him to use. Only through Orcus' direct intervention was Kinst able to create the device, which allowed him to open a portal in the armory (**Area C-4**). Kinst did so and immediately fled to this room. The totem is on a leather thong around Kinst's neck.

Kinst attempts to deceive the characters and says that he is praying for Usis. He acts as if he is ignorant, but he tries to sneak off if combat becomes a possibility. Kinst may also try to give the characters a spare manuscript poisoned with demon's ink, saying that it is a map of the catacombs or other useful information. The manuscript is in the top drawer of his dresser.

A **bone devil** lurks here in the Ethereal Plane. The devil was sent to gather information about the key and the vault. Kinst originally tried to bargain with the devil's master, but did not agree to the devil's "commission" for assisting Kinst. The devil instead sent his spy to infiltrate the Citadel.

The bone devil remains hidden in the Ethereal Plane and does not attack unless provoked. Instead, the spy follows them to gain information about their quest. The details of the adventure's outcome depend on whether or not the spy is still alive by the time the characters leave through the lower archway. Note that the size of the Ethereal Plane here is the same as the Citadel's demiplane. Touching the Ethereal Plane here does not allow one to leave the plane and travel anywhere but on the Citadel's demiplane.

Encounter III-E: The Gate (Area C-5)

This room is the epicenter of the demons' breach. After the *gate* opened here, the demons secured the southern section of the lower level. Currently, the **hezrou** Kainhis is attempting to force her way into taking Galm and the only *portal rune* (see **Appendix A**) that leads to the catacombs. Other occupants include a **vrock** named Tarashix, and a **glabrezu** named Gleegog.

The characters should attempt to close the portal, yet they are under no obligation to do so. If the characters are successful in closing the portal by destroying the *totem of the gate* (see **Encounter III-D** and **Appendix A**), they in effect banish instantaneously every demon who passed through the portal. Reinforcements may arrive through the portal every 15 rounds. Every 15 rounds, roll 1d12 and consult the table below. Note that additional vrocks and hezrous appear only once. If you roll their associated number again, nothing arrives.

1d12	Reinforcement
1–8	Nothing arrives
9	**Dretch**
10	**Succubus**
11	**Vrock**
12	**Hezrou**

Tactics: Gleegog and Tarashix are already bored. Although they had the pleasure of leading the surprise attack into the Citadel, the thrill quickly faded as no real challenge has presented itself. Their current master Orcus whipped the demons into a frenzy when he promised them a river of blood and fresh souls. When they stepped through the portal and saw only a throng of angry dwarves, however, they rolled their eyes and commenced the slaughter. Neither demon can summon any allies due to the magic protecting the Citadel. If Gleegog dies, Tarashix continues to fight, but if the battle seems hopeless, he rushes back through the portal. While Tarashix never negotiates, Gleegog is willing to do anything to reach the portal.

Concluding the Chapter

Once the characters convince King Galm of their intentions (likely through saving the day and defeating the demons and exposing Kinst), he is amenable to giving them the *portal rune* (see **Appendix A**) to the catacombs. Galm has Usis or another priest inscribe the rune above the one used to enter the Citadel. This rune is of Dwurfater's anvil.

Many dwarves openly disagree with Galm's decision to allow the characters into the catacombs. Although the debate is hostile and open, no dwarves make a move to stop the characters. Ultimately, the division over the decision leads to the downfall of the dwarves.

As the characters step through the portal, they travel once against through time and space and enter the catacombs.

CHAPTER FOUR: THE KEY

INTRODUCTORY CHARACTERISTICS

Wandering Monsters: This demiplane is disturbed only when the dwarves bury their dead kings. Due to its isolation, it is not home to many wandering monsters. Check once every 60 minutes on 1d12:

1d12	Encounter
1	The **ghost** of Galm (from **Encounter IV-A**)
2	The **demonvessel** (see **Appendix B**) of Kinst (from **Encounter IV-B**)
3–4	1d6 **corrupted** (from **Encounter IV-C**, see **Appendix B**)
5–12	No encounter

Shielding: Travel spells to the outside are blocked by a similar shielding magic that protects the Citadel (as described in **Chapter Two**).

Detections: The entire area radiates a hint of evil if detection magic is used, due to the corrupted and the demonvessel. **Encounters IV-F** and **IV-G** radiate strong magic.

Standard Features: Unless otherwise noted, all doors are locked, pivot on a central point, and are made of stone. Also, each room is as tall as it is wide, except where otherwise noted. Thus, a majority of hallways in the Citadel are only five feet tall. In these cramped areas, Medium creatures taller than a dwarf are considered to be squeezing (cutting their speed in half and giving them disadvantage on attack rolls and Dexterity saving throws). The entire area is dark.

Map Used: Map D: The Catacombs and Map E: The Key.

The characters enter the catacombs with the *portal rune* (see **Appendix A**) obtained from Galm. Yet instead of sending the characters to a timeline similar to that of the Citadel, strange chaotic energies exerted by the Faceless Lord send the characters many years into the future (relative to the Citadel).

A demiplane created by Dwurfater, the catacombs serve a dual purpose. The first is an actual catacomb for the dead kings of Clan Flammeaxte who lived in the Citadel. The second purpose is to guard the key. The dwarves believe that the spirits of their dead kings exist throughout time as guardians. This function is also to dissuade any visitors into believing that they are actually in the appropriate demiplane with the key.

Thus, the first part of this level houses the tombs. Roughhewn out of granite, the caves are lined with the bodies of the dwarven kings. Some of these rooms have elaborate rune-covered walls emblazoned with gold leaf that list the battles and victories of the dead.

During his first few millennia trapped within his own vault, the Faceless Lord used what small divinity he had to find this demiplane and exert his influence upon it. He believed that doing so might return the key to him. Dwurfater subverted the Faceless Lord's folly by further strengthening the guardians and traps with the Faceless Lord's own slimes and oozes.

In this subversion, the power of the Faceless Lord created a special type of undead, the corrupted. The corrupted are mindless and attack the characters on sight, as described in **Encounters IV-D** and **IV-K**. Two other residents in the tombs of priests and kings are worth noting. One is the ghost of Galm. Years after the characters leave the "Siege of Orcus" era, King Galm, whom the characters met in the Citadel, was assassinated for allowing the characters into the catacombs. Now that the characters are in a different (and future) relative timeframe, they might once again meet Galm.

Galm's ghost laments the division between the dwarves and may become enraged or helpful depending on how the encounter unfolds with the characters in the "Siege of Orcus." Galm holds no ill will about his decision to allow the characters into the catacombs. His torment is that Kinst opened the portal in the first place and that many innocent dwarves lost their lives.

Similarly, a demonvessel is present who may remember the characters. The demonvessel is the remains of Kinst. If Kinst encountered the characters in the "Siege of Orcus" and they foiled his plans, he definitely remembers them and becomes incensed.

Beyond the catacombs is the key complex. A number of oozes and similar creatures are in the complex due to the Faceless Lord's influence. The complex ends in a series of three rooms designed to prevent anyone from obtaining the key.

When he was laid to rest by the new king, Galm entered the catacombs centuries before the characters. Similarly, preceding Galm, Kinst was laid to rest and also entered the catacombs at a different time before the characters.

Encounter IV-A: Ghost of Galm (Area D-1)

A number of burial vaults are sealed and undisturbed along two walls. Intricate stone carvings, presumably of the entombed, adorn the covers of each vault. Some of the carvings show a dwarf in battle; some are of dwarves with large crowns and hideously large smiles on their faces; some are more detailed, with shields and weapons seeming to burst from the stone.

The walls are made of smooth bricks of black rock, like the bricks inside a forge. Soot is everywhere, as if the entire room was ablaze at one point. A few tracks lead from the entrance to a large, life-sized statue in the room's center. A dwarf statue stands high on a dais, holding a battleaxe with two hands and wearing ornate armor with a hammer tied to its belt. The statue seems somehow familiar.

This is one of the tombs containing the remains of kings of the Citadel. The statue is of King Galm. Although vilified for allowing the characters into the catacombs, many dwarves remembered his (presumably) remarkable victory over the demons. A character may recognize the statue if he or she previously encountered King Galm. On the statue are Galm's armor, *+2 battleaxe*, and crown (a simple band of gold with 3 large rubies valued at 2,000 gp each). The spirit of Galm, a **ghost** who can choose to suppress his Horrifying Visage around the characters if he wishes, hides within the statue.

A chill wind emanates from the statue. Galm may speak, blink the statue's eyes, or prepare to strike, depending on how the characters interacted with Galm in the "Siege of Orcus." Galm knows of the key, but does not know of the magical traps. He can direct the characters past the boulder trap (**Encounter IV-C**) and to the secret door leading south. Finally, Galm may ask the characters to help him destroy the "evil one" (Kinst) who torments him. Galm is much more subdued in unlife, but he is still very keen.

Galm desires to be laid to rest. His torment is that Kinst betrayed the dwarves and held a position of such high confidence, and so he blames himself for the lives of the dwarves who died. Furthermore, Galm suspected in life that Kinst was his own son. Galm never confessed his tryst with Kinst's mother to anyone, especially to Kinst's father. Galm always helped Kinst out behind the scenes on the off chance that he was his son, though now he feels that he overlooked the obvious evil in the boy due to his guilt about the adultery, and many dwarves lost their lives as a

consequence. Galm's torment continues as Kinst flourishes and walks in unlife as a demonvessel. Galm now desires that Kinst's soul be extinguished for the evil Kinst caused. Defeating Kinst and returning evidence of his destruction to Galm lays Galm's soul to rest at last, releasing him from unlife.

Encounter IV-B: Demonvessel of Kinst

A soft whispering noise can be heard just ahead. A chill is in the air, and the smell of blood fills your nose. You hear the shuffling of feet and see something dart about up ahead. Around a corner, you see the long cowl of a figure you judge to be a dwarf. A long hand paws at the wall as the figure peers at you. From your vantage, you can see that it wears the robes of a priest and seems to have a long piece of burned wood around its neck.

The figure is Kinst, a **demonvessel** (see **Appendix B**), lamenting his failure to become a powerful lord (his failure might be due to the characters' actions in the Citadel during the "Siege of Orcus"). Kinst's soul is damned to wander the catacombs as a demonvessel. As a mockery, the dwarves laid Kinst to rest as a "king," basically in the hallway of the catacombs, so that throughout time he would lie and see the true kings of the Citadel knowing he would never reach that status.

Hateful and remorseful, Kinst sometimes lurks in the tomb where Galm is buried. He sits upon a vault whispering hateful words and chastising Galm for not showing him the true path, interspersing his dialogue with gleeful gibberish about how he triumphed over Galm.

If the characters dispatched Kinst in the "Siege of Orcus," he may remember them (with a successful DC 15 Intelligence check). A character recognizes Kinst if he or she encountered Kinst previously. Kinst still has the heart of a coward and may flee and attempt to ambush the characters later. Around Kinst's neck is a small totem he made to remind himself of the totem he used to start the "Siege of Orcus."

Kinst wanders constantly and may be found anywhere in the catacombs. You should place him appropriately.

Encounter IV-C: Boulder Trap (Area D-2)

This hallway has a faux ceiling made of plaster that is painted to resemble roughhewn granite. Evenly spaced about the floor are four tripwires made of thin hairs. Stepping on a wire releases one of four boulders concealed in a cavity above the plaster. Each boulder is five feet in diameter.

The hallway is also at a steep incline (30 degrees), so any boulder that falls may roll through other tripwires and trigger more boulders. This is an exceptionally fatal trap if all four boulders are triggered and the majority of the party is standing in front of the first boulder. The trap can be noted by scrutinizing the floor and succeeding on a DC 19 Intelligence (Investigation) check. It can be disarmed with a successful DC 15 Dexterity check with thieves' tools. If a wire is broken without disarming the trap, the character who broke the wire or anyone else who is in the space beneath the boulder must make a DC 17 Dexterity saving throw, taking 27 (5d10) bludgeoning damage on a failure or half as much damage on a success. All creatures in the hallway and downhill from released boulders must also make a DC 14 Dexterity check *for each boulder*, taking 27 (5d10) bludgeoning damage on a failure or half as much damage on a success.

Encounter IV-D: Corrupted (Area D-3)

In this area dwell 6 **corrupted** (see **Appendix B**). They appear to be sick and feverish dwarves. The dwarves are lying in the room's smallish alcoves and appear to be coughing or choking — although, strangely enough, they make no sound. Each of the dwarves wears chainmail and is armed with an axe. Their beards are tangled, and some seem to have a blank stare on their gaunt faces.

These strange dwarves are actually undead creatures known as the corrupted. The characters may mistake the corrupted for living dwarves. The corrupted attack mindlessly as soon as the characters enter the room.

Encounter IV-E: Musical Chairs (Area D-4)

The walls, ceiling, and floor of this room are covered in sheets of beaten copper. Stepping on the floor's edge causes a creak of metal rubbing against stone. At various intervals, the metal is warped, creating a pocket underneath. A five-step dais made of green marble is in the center of the room. A large silver key is in the middle of the dais. A huge blob of slime and goo surrounds the key, and the slime covers the entire dais and overflows onto the floor. The ooze seems to have millions of little crystals in it that reflect light in a prism of colors.

The gooey mass is actually an entity known as a prismatic slime. Because of the size of the dais, the characters may be forced to walk on it as they move around the room. The sticky slime is impervious to any elemental damage such as acid, cold, fire, or even magic, but it can be scraped away and does not damage any tool used to remove it. The slime and the key are merely decoys. If two characters are

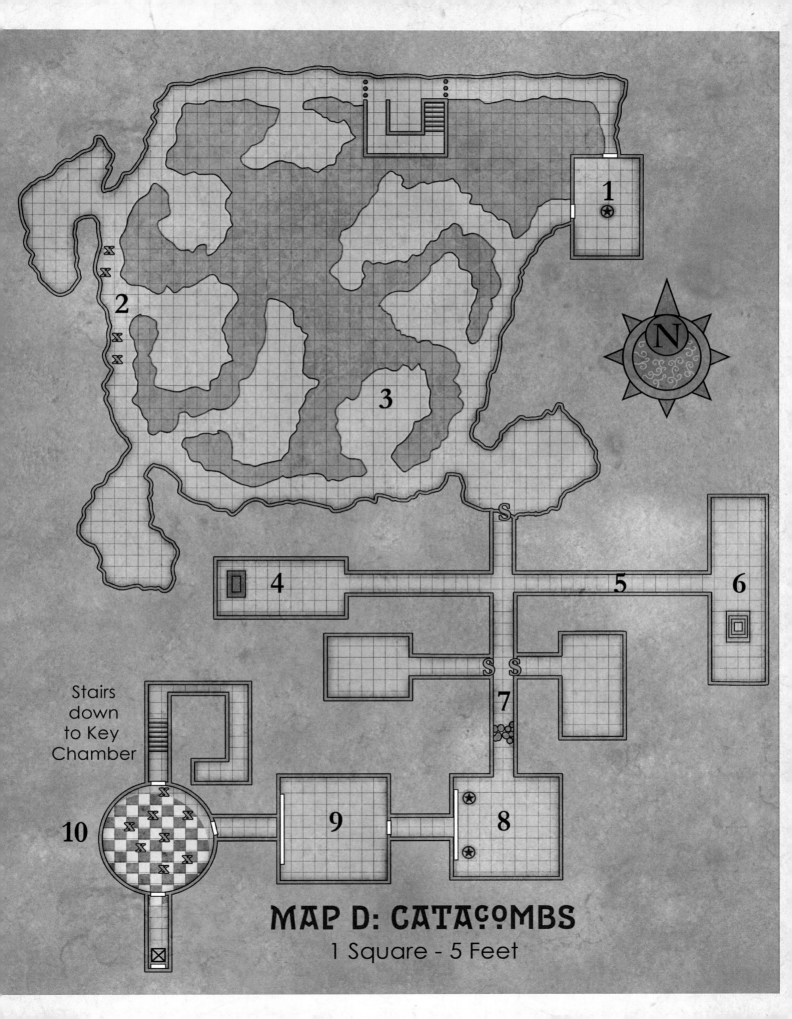

1

2

3

N

4

5

6

7

Stairs
down
to Key
Chamber

10

9

8

MAP D: CATACOMBS
1 Square - 5 Feet

standing on the dais at the same time, each of them must make a DC 15 Charisma saving throw. If one characters fails or if they both succeed, there is no effect. If two fail, they effectively switch bodies (i.e., their psyches trade places so that they find themselves within the other's body). The players should trade character record sheets. The switched characters have access to all of their new host body's physical attributes, but mental abilities (such as spellcasting) do not transfer.

The transference lasts until the curse is removed by a *remove curse* (cast using a 5th level slot or higher), a *wish*, or a similar spell. In the meantime, it should make for interesting role-playing, especially when the wizard goes charging into battle with his dagger and the mighty barbarian scratches his head wondering where his *wand of magic missiles* is! If multiple characters step onto the dais at the same time, simply match the pairs randomly. The entire party could possibly be switched. Stepping on the dais again does not trigger a reverse effect.

ENCOUNTER IV-F: CRAWLING UP THE WALL (AREA D-5)

Along this hallway is a **livestone** (see **Appendix B**), one of the Faceless Lord's creations. This large ooze has formed the sidewalls and ceiling, and it now yearns for prey. Once a majority of the characters are under it, the livestone attacks and attempts to engulf the party.

ENCOUNTER IV-G: SLIME VS. SLIME (AREA D-6)

This room is similar to **Area D-1**. One of the vaults, however, is full of ooze. The center vault or crypt contains a dormant **mustard jelly** (see **Appendix B**) that awakens at the first vibration (e.g. a sound, a footstep) from anyone entering the room. Another dormant ooze, a **stun jelly** (see **Appendix B**), is on the ceiling. This nearly transparent ooze covers the area of the ceiling opposite the crypt containing the mustard jelly. If the crypt is disturbed and opened, the stun jelly senses movement and drops onto the victims and/or the floor to attack. The oozes are semi-aware of each other and realize that neither is as tasty as the characters' flesh.

ENCOUNTER IV-H: STONE PORTAL (AREA D-7)

The hallway ends abruptly. A large stone barrier here blocks further access. The barrier seems to be a large block of granite, and in its center is the Dwarvish rune for death. Surrounding the rune are many warnings carved or painted onto the stone. The warnings read, "Do not enter. Grave danger!" and "Only evil seeks what is within!"

A five-foot cube of granite blocks the path down to the key. The characters must dig or mine through the cube to gain access below. There is nothing unusual about the granite; magic affects it as per standard stone.

If the **demonvessel** (see **Appendix B**) survived up to this point, he ambushes the characters here. In any event, the mining, loud noises, or even spellcasting awakens a vile **vampiric ooze** (see **Appendix B**). The ooze long ago found refuge in a small space above the stone barrier. As soon as someone begins to pound on the rock, the yellowish ooze slips out of this area and flows down the face of the rock. The ooze has not found a decent morsel to consume since it found itself here eons ago. It attacks relentlessly due to its unnatural hunger.

ENCOUNTER IV-I: CHIMERA GATE (AREA D-8)

Dust hangs heavy in the air. The floor is black marble, crossed by small bars of silver. The ceiling high above is painted and shows a great battle. A picture of a large black cube that sits on a representation of the Devil's Finger is on the north wall. Above the cube is a vortex of swirling color with hundreds of red eyes, and a demon army is shooting out of the black cube like a ray. A picture of a seething dwarf striking a hammer against an anvil is on the south wall. The dwarf has black hair and large brown eyes; his teeth flash white as he grits them. From the anvil, a spray of dwarves shoots forth and meets the painted demons in combat. To the west, a gigantic 15-foot-tall circular door stands closed. A large tablet with numerous runes on it is in the center of the door. Two large statues of three-headed beasts with the bodies of lions stand on either side of the door. The statues' stony paws are made to look as if they are swiping at each other. Their other paws are raised, ready to strike anyone standing before the door.

This room is the first of three traps designed to protect the key. Each room is 30 feet tall and has carvings showing the evil works of the Faceless Lord on the north side with the good works of Dwurfater on the south. On the far side is a large 15-foot-tall circular door. You may wish to copy the tablet's inscription to hand to the players. The tablet in the center of the door reads as follows in ancient Dwarvish:

> Call forth the chaos!
> Time lost he came to the shores of this world.
> Defeated by the hand of dwarf.
> His amulet is what you seek.
> Go away! Go away!
> Desire it, love it, hate it, make merry.
> Take the eyes of the guardians, multiply by their feet, and subtract their scaled heads.
> Speak the number of the enemy in the tongue of the enemy.

The statues are actually **chimeras**. They attack as soon as any character approaches within 10 feet of the door or answers the door riddle incorrectly. One of the chimeras has its Fire Breath trait replaced with:

Acid Breath (recharge 5–6). The dragon head exhales acid in a 15-foot cone. Each creature in that area must make a DC 15 Dexterity saving throw, taking 31 (7d8) acid damage on a failed save, or half as much on a successful one.

To open the door, the characters must say the number "86" in Abyssal. The solution is 11 eyes (one chimera has 5 eyes, and the other has 6) times 8 feet (4 on each chimera) minus 2 scaled heads (2 dragon heads) (11 x 8 – 2 = 86). The characters might not notice that the black dragon head on one chimera is missing an eye. The characters should specifically state that they are looking at the heads to notice this fact. Any answer that is incorrect or spoken in a language other than Abyssal activates the chimera.

Also, the characters cannot "divine" an answer through magical means. The magical enchantments of the Citadel prevent access to planes of evil. Furthermore, good-aligned planes and deities cannot answer in Abyssal, for it is the language of evil, and have little use for those seeking to obtain (no matter the purpose) a demon prince's amulet. The characters must determine the answer on their own without outside assistance. Finally, *knock* spells do not function on the lock.

To make this encounter difficult, do not allow the players access to a calculator or other device. Allow players only one round to write down any calculation, and do not allow them to continue until their turn. This is to simulate the difficulty of calculating an answer while in the midst of combat.

The chimeras return to their stasis only if the lock is successfully opened. If the chimeras are killed, they disappear and reappear as statues in the alcove five minutes later. Thereafter, they attack again if the lock cannot be opened.

Tactics: The larger chimera has a red dragon head and breathes fire. The smaller chimera has a black dragon head and breathes acid. Since both creatures are under a magical influence, they attack unremittingly. Each uses its breath weapon as often as possible, and both concentrate on a different enemy.

ENCOUNTER IV-J: NASAL JELLIES (AREA D-9)

This room is completely bare. Unlike the previous room and hallway, the walls in this room are smooth. Painted on the 30-foot-high ceiling and walls are a swirl of blood red, filth brown, and putrid green colors. Large fist-sized red gems are embedded in the walls and ceiling. The room is full of dust. Particles of dust glint in your [light source]. Across from the door through which you entered is an identical 15-foot-tall circular door with another large tablet in the center.

The room is a perfect cube of smooth stone. For every round the characters spend in the room, they must make a DC 15 Constitution saving throw, with failure meaning that a characters sneezes with tremendous force. The character must immediately make another identical saving throw or be subject to the effects of a *feeblemind* spell. The product of each sneeze appears in an unoccupied square within 10 feet of the character as a small **ochre jelly**. The process repeats itself each round until the characters leave the room.

Proceeding will not be easy, however. You may wish to copy the tablet's inscription to hand to the players. The tablet in the center of this door reads as follows in ancient Dwarvish:

Persistence.

You desire evil and evil you shall bring if you continue.

Chaos abhors order as order brings righteousness to the natural state.

One of chaos came and was defeated.

Shall you be as well?

Desiring chaos and evil now, you shall be one with it.

Speak forth the answer to the following in the tongue of evil:

What is the end of chaos?

The start of swords,

The beginning of every secret,

And the end of the lords?

As soon as a character comes within 10 feet of the inscription, the ceiling begins lowering at a rate of one foot per round. After 18 rounds, the ceiling crushes all who remain in the room. Once the inscription is read, begin counting off rounds aloud to give players a sense of urgency to solve the riddle. If the characters fail to solve the riddle or retreat in a minute and a half, they are crushed. When the ceiling reaches the floor, the room remains in this state until the end of the adventure, effectively blocking the way to the key.

The answer in Abyssal is the letter "S." If this is said aloud, the ceiling returns to its full height. As with the previous encounter, the characters cannot "divine" an answer through spells or some other means. Basically, the characters must determine the answer on their own without outside assistance.

ENCOUNTER IV-K: THE SLICER (AREA D-10)

Each of the doors in this room is hexagonal and seven feet in diameter. Each of the hexagons has faces carved and painted on it: one face is a dwarven visage with a horned helmet and a long beard; the other face has no lips, ears, or nose, but has dozens of painted red eyes. On the walls near the "dwarf door" is a depiction of a great army of skeletons flowing up a valley toward the Devil's Finger. The scene shows a cowled figure raising his hand in triumph, with many dwarven bodies on the ground around him. The scene in the next panel on the door shows dwarves being torn apart by undead and the cowled figure lying prone and bleeding on the ground. The last panel shows a spirit rising from the cowled figure. The spirit is very tall, with cold blue eyes, and it shakes its hands in rage at the heavens. The undead about it seem to walk aimlessly around the Devil's Finger.

The walls by the faceless door show a boar-headed demon driving a horde toward the Devil's Finger. The next scene depicts the boar-headed demon talking to a dwarf, followed by the image of the dwarf waving a wand and demons appearing in front of him. The next panel shows the dwarf being hung in the Citadel's main hall. The last panel shows a spirit of the evil dwarf rising up in the form of a gray creature holding an arm over his head to shield its face from the glory of a stoic dwarven deity.

The floor of the room is made up of black and white marble squares. Grooves are visible around each tile. A large brass key suspended by a wire from the ceiling is in the center of the room. Surrounding the key are several motionless dwarves. They seem to be perspiring profusely despite the fact that they are not moving.

This room has stonework unlike any other section of the Citadel. Instead of seamless stone, this area is made of marble tiles set apart with deep groves between them. Lengths of razor-sharp wire rest in the grooves. Pressure plates (denoted by an "X" on Map D) trigger the wires and cause them to rise rapidly, slicing into the foot of anyone standing on the grooves. Inspecting the floor and succeeding on a DC 14 Intelligence (Investigation) check allows a character to notice the trap. It can be disarmed with a successful DC 15 Dexterity check with thieves' tools. Anyone stepping on a pressure plate must make a DC 16 Dexterity saving throw, being sliced by the wire and taking 10 (3d6) slashing damage on a failure or half as much on a success.

The dwarves — a gang of 8 corrupted (see Appendix B) — immediately attack the characters once they enter the room. The corrupted know of the pressure plates and put two of their members in position to activate them at opportune times.

The key is a fake. If any character touches the key, it turns to dust, and a magic mouth activates. The magic mouth laughs and says in Dwarvish, "You did not think it would be that easy, did you?" Once the key is touched, two doors open to reveal two different passageways. The only way to open the doors is by touching the fake key. One door opens to reveal a hallway, at the end of which is a gold-embossed door. This is a false door, and in front of it is an 80-foot-deep pit trap. The trap can be detected with an examination of the floor and a successful DC 15 Intelligence (Investigation) check and disarmed with a successful DC 13 Dexterity check with thieves' tools. Creatures who trigger the trap must make a DC 16 Dexterity saving throw, falling in the pit and taking 28 (8d6) bludgeoning damage on a failure. The other door leads to a stairwell down to the true key.

ENCOUNTER IV-L: THE KEY ROOM (MAP E)

The long stairway ends abruptly in a smooth stone landing. Beyond the landing is a room with its own light source. The landing, however, drops off into a chasm, the depth of which is impossible to estimate.

The room itself is large and round. The ceiling is 50 feet high at its apex, rounded like a dome. In the center of the room is a large column that begins from the darkness below and ends 10 feet above the landing. The column is almost 40 feet from the landing's edge.

The source of the light is a large anvil atop the pillar. The anvil sits on a three-step dais on the pillar's summit and fills the room with a silvery light. It looks to be made of silver or platinum. Even from this distance, you can tell that hundreds of intricate black runes cover the anvil. Flanking the anvil are two metal statues of 10-foot-tall dwarves, both of them armed with large axes and posed as if they were in combat.

The anvil is the key. It is made of pure platinum, weighs 500 pounds, and is worth 250,000 gp based on the value of the metal alone. The anvil emits a pale light to 50 feet in all direction. It also radiates a 25-foot antimagic field, which is a permanent effect. The characters must rely on their wits and natural abilities instead of magic in order to obtain the key. They must deal with this cumbersome challenge until they open the vault and the anvil teleports back to this location. Any spells cast within the sphere fail automatically. Furthermore, all wondrous items and magic abilities within the sphere are suppressed.

The statues on each side of the key are 2 iron golems. The golems are both within the antimagic field. This means that they, like the anvil, cannot be the targets of a magical attack. This also means that they can be struck by normal weapons while within the field. They are still animated, however, and otherwise function normally.

If an unknowing character approaches the key with magical aid (such as a fly spell), the spell shuts down as soon as the character passes into the antimagic field. Since this is a demiplane, anyone falling into the chasm falls for eternity. Anyone who successfully reaches the key is attacked by the golems, which were ordered long ago to protect the key at all costs. Once the golems are eliminated as a threat, the characters must come up with a non-magical, mundane means of removing the key, such as rigging a block-and-tackle system.

To complicate this issue, the dwarves engineered certain areas around the column to break away if anyone should land on them. Anyone over 50 pounds in the shaded area on Map E must roll below their dexterity on 4d6 or fall into the chasm.

Tactics: The golems attempt to grab characters and throw the victims over the edge.

CONCLUDING THE CHAPTER

Once the characters have the key, they must trek back to the portal from whence they came. Moving the key should be a very difficult challenge. First, it weighs 500 pounds; second, it is a beacon of light; third, it creates an antimagic field in a 25-foot radius. Although many of the guardians and monsters in the catacombs might be defeated, the challenges in "Necromantic Dreams" are even harder with this burden.

Once the characters reach the portal, they can use it even though it is within the antimagic field, for the portal's source for its magic is not in proximity to the key. Thus, the characters can step through with the key — and hopefully, surprisingly for them — not return to the "Siege of Orcus" but to the nightmarish "Necromantic Dreams."

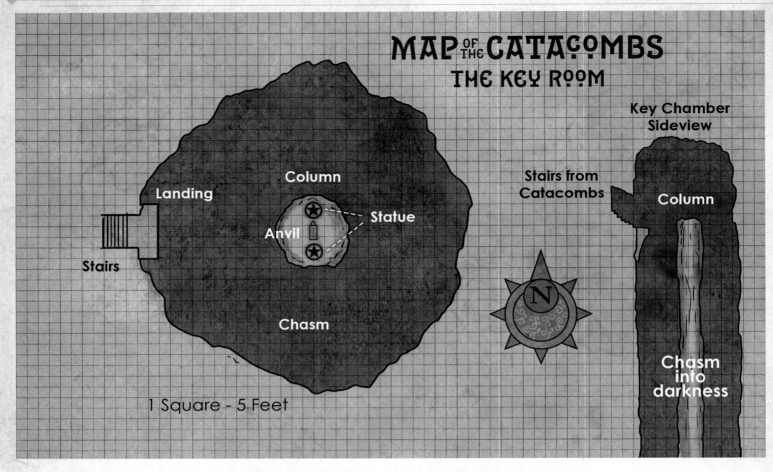

CHAPTER FIVE:
ASCENT - NECROMANTIC DREAMS

INTRODUCTORY CHARACTERISTICS

Wandering Monsters: The entire Citadel is now abandoned. Only the remnants of an army of undead occupy the fortress. Check every 30 minutes on a 1d12.

1d12	Encounter
1	Giltz, the **dark custodian** (see **Appendix B**) from **Encounter V-A**
2	The **vampires** from **Encounter V-E**
3	Roaming pack of 2d4 **mummies**
4	2d4 **ghasts** and 1d6 + 6 **ghouls**
5–6	One of the NPC parties from **Chapter Two**
7–12	No encounter

Shielding: Teleportation or travel outside the Citadel in any form is impossible, as previously described.

Detections: The characters detect a minor evil throughout the Citadel if detection magic is used. The Temple (**Area C-6**) radiates a strong evil because it has been thoroughly defiled by Giltz.

Standard Features: Unless otherwise noted, all doors are on a central pivot and made of stone. Since the Citadel was carved out of the granite of the Devil's Finger, the floor, walls, and ceiling are seamless. The rock is polished smooth and has a mirror-like quality; also, every noise echoes throughout the stone structure. Both of these qualities of the Citadel's environment make sneaking about or hiding very difficult Characters have disadvantage on Dexterity (Stealth) checks. On the other hand, the echo effect makes it easier for a party to hear what is ahead and around the bend. Also, each room is as tall as wide, except where otherwise noted. Thus, a majority of hallways in the Citadel are only five feet tall. In these cramped areas, Medium creatures taller than a dwarf are considered to be squeezing (cutting their speed in half and giving them disadvantage on attack rolls and Dexterity saving throws). The entire area is dark.

Maps Used: Map B: The Citadel — The Upper Halls; Map C: The Citadel — The Lower Halls

Returning from the events of **Chapter Four**, the characters enter the lower archway and travel through time to 1,200 years before the "present" on their home plane. Coming back through the archway, the characters may anticipate that they are returning to the vibrant time of Galm with a siege of demons and dwarves running about to defend the Citadel. Or perhaps they are the heroes of the Citadel, and getting back to the upper archway should be an easy trek …

This anticipation is shattered when they return through the archway and enter the Citadel's demiplane in another era. Thus, the characters must reinvestigate many chambers they previously explored, as these areas are populated with a fresh slate of foes. If this proves too difficult a task for certain parties, tailor the encounters to match the characters' resources.

The events of "Necromantic Dreams" occur more than a century after the last dwarves to occupy the Citadel were slaughtered by an army of undead commanded by the necromancer Giltz, who learned through his studies that the Citadel held the key and the means to access it. Inscribing the *portal rune* (see **Appendix A**) on his undead minions, he brought his host of undead against the dwarves.

The dwarves at the time were in a period of decline. Many of them had left the Citadel for their ancestral homes. Others felt that there was no longer a need to defend a key that seemed to be more myth than threat. Moreover, the work of the Cabal of the Beard had decimated the dwarves' strength. So, when Giltz arrived, he did not face a fully defended stronghold.

The final dwarven defenders made a trap for Giltz. Though dying in the process, the dwarves struck a mortal blow to the priest. Upon his death, Giltz's animosity and anger for his failure at the doorstep of success was so great and his debt to the powers of death so large that he now roams the Citadel as a dark custodian. The characters must face Giltz to enter the upper archway. If they have the key with them, Giltz brings whatever forces he can against the characters.

We highly recommend that two or more parties of NPCs described in **Chapter Two** be placed in this era. One group is the Cabal of the Beard, which was sent forward in time to take the key from the characters. Persuading the cabal to join forces with the characters is possible, especially if another NPC group is attempting to acquire or already has acquired the key.

Another group recommended for this era is the Brotherhood of the Ooze. The members of the brotherhood are fanatical devotees of the Faceless Lord who are ineptly searching for the key. Basically, the brotherhood is a band of bumbling dolts intended to bring a bit of levity to the adventure. The brotherhood is wary of Giltz and might join forces with the characters to destroy him. The brotherhood immediately takes the key if possible, though.

You could also easily place the mercenary Imbo, the devil-following Silver Eyes (who possibly received information about the characters from the bone devil spy), or even Raob and Sleeara. In any event, you must know your party's strengths and weaknesses. Using these NPCs is important, but only where the characters stand a chance; otherwise, they are overkill and not fun.

One eventuality is that an NPC acquires and leaves the Citadel with the key. Make anyone leaving the Citadel return to the characters' present time, including the cabal. Thus, the characters must fight in and around the Devil's Finger in the time up to the blood moon. Due to the strange temporal nature of the archways, the characters and the NPCs return 10 days before the blood moon. This should be plenty of time to reacquire a key from those desiring a cataclysm of evil.

Other than Giltz and any NPCs you place, the other Citadel residents are various undead who are also driven by their thirst to extinguish life. Shadow mastiffs constantly hunt the infrequent visitor or adventuring party (**Encounter V-B**). Specters of dwarven craftsmen continue to work on jewelry and metalworking, even though they can no longer craft their work (**Encounter V-C**). A band of allips (**Encounter V-D**), shades of long-dead dwarves bemoaning the loss of the Citadel, harbor a deep-seated hate of those who attempt to make it their home. Finally, there is a pair of vain vampires (**Encounter V-E**).

ENCOUNTER V-A: GILTZ THE DARK CUSTODIAN (AREA B-1)

Pain and remorse are Giltz's hallmarks. He inflicted both upon his enemies in life. Now in unlife, he knows nothing but these two emotions. The last dwarves sacrificed themselves to slay him, and his great anguish at the time of his defeat propels him forward.

Giltz is a **dark custodian** (see **Appendix B**; dwarves are the subject of Giltz's Directed Hatred ability) and may be encountered as a wandering monster because he constantly moves about. The dark custodian must squeeze in low hallways (cutting his speed in half and giving him disadvantage on attack rolls and Dexterity saving throws). Giltz has retained most of the cruel intelligence of his former life. Constantly seething with anger over his failure, Giltz's only freedom from remorse and regret is the momentary distraction of squeezing the life out of others. It is extraordinarily unlikely that the characters will be able to communicate with Giltz, especially if he encounters the characters with the Cabal of the Beard. Dwarves drive Giltz into a froth, and he stops at nothing to see them destroyed. Giltz wanders a bit, but if he sees the key, he might station himself at the upper portal, blocking it with his mass if necessary.

Giltz is aware of other intruders, such as other NPC parties, but elects to allow them to wander a bit to make a sport of their deaths. The characters are treated differently if they have the key.

Tactics: Giltz plays with the characters unless one of them is a dwarf, he recognizes the key, or if they are teamed with the Cabal of the Beard. Giltz tries to eliminate a member in each attack and attacks if the party is engaged with another foe.

ENCOUNTER V-B: GHOST DOGS OF WAR (AREA B-1)

The once great entry hall to the Citadel lies in ruins. Tattered standards and ripped banners hang from the high ceiling and move slightly in the heavy air. Carvings once proclaimed, "Welcome Friends!" and "Death to Fiends!" Gleeful at taking the Citadel, prior to his death Giltz had his minions paint over the carvings so that they read "Welcome Fiends!" and "Death to Friends!"

In this room are 4 **shadow mastiffs**. When the characters enter, pools of viscous liquid form in the middle of the room. The liquid spills down from a source that seems to be floating in midair — what appear to be two sets of canine teeth. The teeth belong to two of the shadow mastiffs.

At one time, these creatures were Giltz's personal pets. They now guard the entrance into the Citadel (and the characters' exit). Two of the shadow mastiffs are in the center of the room. The other two are in opposite hallways preparing to flank the party.

Tactics: The shadow mastiffs track the characters if they flee. Each mastiff alternates between baying and attacking. If he is not already present, there is a 25% chance of Giltz being drawn to the room each time a mastiff bays.

ENCOUNTER V-C: SPECTERS OF THE PAST (AREA B-3)

Unlike other parts of the Citadel in this era, this room does not seem to be in disrepair. It contains numerous wooden benches and tables, and near its center is a large brazier that has probably sat cold for over a hundred years.

At some of the tables, wispy images of dwarves sit staring at large pieces of platinum and ruby jewelry. One of these incorporeal dwarves puts his hand through the table, and another is sobbing softly to himself.

This is a workshop for jewelers whose pieces funded the Citadel for more than 1,000 years. In the characters' home plane, these works of art are very valuable.

The dwarves are 4 specters. Interestingly, each specter still longs to work on the last object that remained incomplete during its life. Although their incorporeal hands can no longer shape the stone and metal, if this fact is brought to their attention, they grow angry with the reminder. In other words, a character blurting out anything similar to "Don't they know they are specters?" or "What idiots! They can't work those forges!" sends the spectres into a frenzy as their grief drives them mad. Anyone examining their wares also incurs their wrath.

These specters were dwarves who refused to get up from their tables and fight when Giltz attacked. Their longing for perfection kept them here endlessly attempting to work on the items they cannot touch.

Treasure: The specters are working on seven pieces of jewelry. They are brocades of platinum and large rings with rubies. Each item is worth 1,000 gp.

ENCOUNTER V-D: BEMOANING THE PAST (AREA B-9)

This room was cleared of its belongings to form a blockade prior to a skirmish during the siege. As the characters approach, however, they hear the present occupants: a ravening pack of 5 **allips** (see **Appendix B**). The allips constantly bemoan their suffering, speaking mournfully in an ancient Dwarvish dialect. As previously mentioned, these are the shades of dwarves who died defending the Citadel against Giltz.

ENCOUNTER V-E: LOVE, UNDEAD STYLE

Even evil needs a reprieve. The two lieutenants of the host of undead led by Giltz were very unusual. One was a woman named Tenear (a **vampire** with a *+1 dagger*).

Appearance: Tenear has long red hair that reaches almost to her knees. She wears a simple gown of blue satin. From the back of the gown emerge two large, bluish bat wings. She has two small black horns that protrude from her forehead. She is incredibly beautiful … in the darkest sort of way.

The other was a man named Zaitan, who also uses the statistics of a **vampire**.

Appearance: Zaitan is very handsome. He has black hair that he keeps very short, small black horns, and black wings. He wears a simple red doublet over his milk-white skin.

Tenear was a victim of a union between a foul demon and a beautiful nymph. Strikingly beautiful in life, she hid her bat-like wings and small horns under cloaks and long bangs. Living the life of a highway bandit and later a baroness of a small cadre of criminals, her notoriety grew. Unfortunately, this notoriety attracted the attention of Zaitan, a darker agent of evil.

Zaitan seduced the vile Tenear with his unearthly charms. Once a demon and now undead, Zaitan remembers little of the circumstances of his rebirth. His desire for the opposite sex was ravenous, though. Many ladies fell victim to his deadly kiss. Although satisfying, Zaitan desired something more.

Tenear caught Zaitan's eye. He was enraptured by her striking beauty and unusual parentage. He desired her and did not wish to simply rob her of life. The Abyss was no place for the likes of Tenear. Zaitan devised a plan and through his wiles soon had Tenear swooning for him. At the right moment, he granted her the dark gift. Ever since this union, the two have been mutually enraptured with one another and their stunning and dark beauty.

Coming to the call of Giltz, Tenear and Zaitan were the advance guard against the dwarves. When Giltz died, Tenear and Zaitan returned to their favorite pastime of admiring one another. The demon's amulet and the power that comes with it mean very little to the pair. Since the day Giltz died, the two vampires find each other's company intoxicating. They do their best to avoid their tormented former master.

If the characters encounter these stunning and unusual creatures, they politely ask the characters to leave them be. Although they hunger, the two frequently leave the Citadel's demiplane and hunt since they both have the appropriate rune. If the characters persist in asking questions, the pair is likely to send them away with their Charm rather than attack. Basically, they view anyone with a Charisma score less than 18 as a repulsive peasant.

Only if openly provoked do the two bring their full powers to bear. The two have very little in the way of treasure, as they have little use for material items.

CONCLUDING THE CHAPTER

Assuming the characters bypass or defeat Giltz and the various NPC parties and do not incur the wrath of Tenear and Zaitan, they return to their home plane through the upper archway. At this point, they have 10 days to prepare for the blood moon. Although many days have passed to them, relatively few have passed in the outside world.

If Sleeara and Raob were not dealt with previously, they must be now. In the interim, Raob has possibly given up and moved his army away, believing that the key never existed after spending days tunneling into nothing but granite. In any event, in 10 days, the blood moon rises and with it, chaos.

CHAPTER SIX:
THE PRINCE OF SLIME

INTRODUCTORY CHARACTERISTICS

Shielding: No spells of any kind can penetrate the vault (**Area A-7**). Nothing can damage or see beyond its jet-black obsidian walls. Ancient magical protections prevent anyone from traversing through the Astral Plane in and around the Citadel and the top of the Devil's Finger. Thus, astral travel and teleportation are impossible on, within, or 500 yards around the Devil's Finger. Within the vault, magic of the following kinds does not function (whether it is from a spell or a magic item):

Magic which summons or conjures beings from other planes or elsewhere on this plane.

Magic which provides instantaneous transportation of any kind.

Magic which contacts or obtains information from deities or other planes.

wish (some exceptions noted below)

Detections: Characters who use detection magic detect strong evil and overwhelming magic from the vault (**Area A-7**) due to the presence of the Faceless Lord and his amulet. Also, the Devil's Finger itself radiates moderate magical energies. Within the vault, there is overwhelming evil and magic.

Map Used: Map E: The Vault

After obtaining the key, the characters must use it to enter the vault and obtain the demon's amulet. Retrieving the demon's amulet, however, shall be much more difficult than they could imagine. In some ways, their adventure is just now beginning.

The characters may have learned that the vault also contains the Prince of Slime, the Faceless Lord. They may have discovered this from Galm, Usis, the carvings in the Citadel, the *painting of enlightenment* (see **Appendix A**), or deduced it themselves. Since they had 14 days to complete their mission, they may only have 10 days remaining to prepare for the confrontation with the Faceless Lord's avatar.

The characters might also need to deal with Lord Raob and his army, either through the guerrilla tactics of slowly weeding out the army or simply by driving Raob off. Alternatively, Raob and Sleeara might take the key, and the characters must deal with them once the vault is opened.

On the 14th day in the characters' relative home plane after starting the adventure, a blood moon rises in the east as the sun sets, casting the entire area in a crimson glow. When this event occurs, stairs and a round door appear in the vault's east side. In the center of the door is an anvil-shaped depression into which the key must be placed. Once this is done, blue-hued lightning covers the entire vault. When the vault is opened, the immensely valuable key is teleported back to its residing area in the catacomb demiplane. This is permissible through the shielding of that plane because the anvil is the key. Thereafter, a door opens into the interior.

Once the door is opened, a blast of hot, moist air issues from the vault as the obsidian door swings inward. Below the door are a number of steps leading down to a small stone landing, and beyond the landing a sea of slime rolls as far as the eye can see. Geysers of slime spout globs of sludge into the air. The door has opened into a different plane, for it is impossible that this great sea could fit inside the vault.

About 100 feet beyond the landing is a large island of white sand. Bones of all shapes, sizes, and colors litter the island. At one end is a 200-foot-tall gold cube, featureless like the obsidian vault.

The interior of the vault is supernatural. Apparently, those who walk through the door stand in the middle of a gigantic rolling slime ocean. The walls of the vault are not visible. Yet anyone who approaches the walls or ceiling is rebuffed by a magical force. The doorway in which the characters stand is in midair, 40 feet above the slime.

The ocean is a myriad of purple, orange, and black slimes and oozes. The slime is caustic and functions as if it were **green slime** (see **Appendix B**). Characters are also at risk of drowning in the turbulent ocean.

A sandy island rises in the middle of the slime ocean. A small surf of slime rolls onto the island's shores. The island is featureless except for a large 200-foot-square gold cube supported by numerous eight-foot-tall stone pillars.

The entire area radiates overwhelming evil because the Faceless Lord lurks below the slime, attempting to ascertain the characters' intentions. The Faceless Lord is compelled to protect the amulet due to the power Dwurfater used to trap him. Yet he will not appear to the characters until their intentions are known.

The Faceless Lord is well prepared for those seeking his amulet. Although compelled by Dwurfater to protect the amulet, he has done so in a way that amuses him.

In his solitude, the Faceless Lord took the souls of the dwarves who perished and became trapped with him inside the cube. He used their souls to craft four alternate sub-planes. These sub-planes within this demiplane form a never-ending amusement for the Faceless Lord as he tortures the souls. If the characters desire the amulet, they must overcome the worst the Faceless Lord can offer.

A hollow shaft is in the center of the gold cube, and in this shaft is a large green and white marble obelisk. The top of the obelisk barely crests the top of the cube. Within the obelisk is the Faceless Lord's amulet. To open the obelisk, a riddle must be solved, but in order to read the riddle, the characters must first collect it.

Three of the obelisk's four sides are covered with intricate gold runes. The north side reads in Dwarvish: *He who seeks misery and decay shall find it by speaking the solution!* The south side reads in Elvish (a hatred tongue of dwarves): *Speak the solution to the riddle and misery shall awaken!* The east side reads in Abyssal: *Return the tables and answer the question and paradise is yours!* The west side is bare. Four large four-foot-by-four-foot square plates are visibly missing on the west side. A frame stone around each plate shows where the plate should be placed. The highest plate is 100 feet off the ground, and the lowest plate it 30 feet up. Four symbols are in the back of the plate.

A circular stone platform that encompasses most of the area beneath the cube is beneath the obelisk. Thirteen large openings are in the stone, some on the ceiling and others on the floor. Around each circular opening are stones with the same marking. Each opening has a different marking.

The stone circles are openings to shafts that lead straight down. Each circle is coated with a different color of slime. Only those circles with the correct markings corresponding to the symbols on the obelisk lead somewhere. The other circles and shafts lead to almost certain death. The characters must intentionally jump into the shafts. The walls of the shafts are slippery, but the characters can brace themselves to climb out of the shaft. You are encouraged to create symbols for the 13 circles.

THE THIRTEEN CIRCLES

The 13 circles and where they lead are detailed below:

CIRCLE ONE

This circle is an incorrect choice. The shaft goes 300 feet straight down and radiates some heat. Anyone falling down the shaft takes 70 (20d6) bludgeoning damage. At the end of the shaft is a furnace that is turned on every other day. Anyone in the shaft when the furnace is turned on (50% chance) takes 35 (10d6) fire damage per round.

CIRCLE TWO

The circle is a correct choice. It leads to a sub-plane of your choosing, possibly the Slime Hole sub-plane described below. The cover of the shaft has a bubble of brown liquid that seems ready to pop. The cover acts as a membrane that allows any character to pass through but not pierce the membrane. After falling 150 feet, the character moves through a portal to the Slime Hole demiplane.

CIRCLE THREE

This circle is an incorrect choice. It is above the characters on the ceiling, and a pool of bluish slime drips from the sides of the shaft onto the stone floor. As a character moves beneath the circle, he or she begins to *levitate* up toward the shaft. After two rounds, characters enter the shaft itself and begin to accelerate as they are pulled by a permanent effect similar to a *reverse gravity* spell. The shaft ends after 200 feet. Characters slam into the dead-end and take 70 (20d6) bludgeoning damage.

CIRCLE FOUR

This circle is an incorrect choice. A mound of black ooze pours out of it. The ooze is actually a semi-dormant **black pudding** just waiting for characters to willingly jump into it. The black pudding refuses to move from its shaft. The shaft itself is only 10 feet long.

CIRCLE FIVE

This circle is a correct choice. It leads to a sub-plane of your choosing, possibly the Ogre Rocks sub-plane described below. The shaft is coated with a thick stone-colored slime that looks like gray ooze; however, it is harmless. After falling 200 feet, a characters moves through a portal to the Ogre Rocks demiplane.

CIRCLE SIX

This circle is an incorrect choice. Like Circle Three, this circle is on the ceiling and has active *levitate* and *reverse gravity* effects. The walls of the shaft drip white ooze. Halfway up the shaft are 3 consecutive **gelatinous cubes**. The cubes almost certainly completely envelop any character being pulled along the shaft.

CIRCLE SEVEN

This circle is an incorrect choice. On the ground, this circle has a purplish slime that completely fills the shaft. The slime itself is harmless; however, the shaft widens to 40 feet in diameter after five feet. Furthermore, the slime acts like quicksand, is very difficult to swim or tread in, and subjects characters sinking in it to drowning.

CIRCLE EIGHT

This circle is an incorrect choice. On the ground, this circle's crimson slime seems to bleed. The shaft is 300 feet long and ends in many jagged pieces of crystal. These crystal shards are covered by eight feet of blood. Any character falling down the shaft takes 70 (20d6) bludgeoning damage and lands on 1d6+1 shards that deal 2 (1d4) piercing damage each.

CIRCLE NINE

This circle in the ceiling is a correct choice. It leads to a sub-plane of your choosing, possibly the Asteroid demiplane described below. Like Circle Three, this one has active *levitate* and *reverse gravity* effects. The shaft is full of a foamy brown liquid. While the foam is harmless, some of it floats up along the shaft. Midway along the 100-foot shaft is a portal to the Asteroid demiplane.

CIRCLE TEN

This circle is an incorrect choice. In the floor, this shaft seems devoid of slime. However, anyone moving a majority of his or her body over the ledge triggers a trap from above. A small portal opens in the ceiling and releases 100 gallons of **green slime** (see **Appendix B**) directly down the shaft. Succeeding on a DC 20 Intelligence (Investigation) check allows a character to discern this trap. If a character can get up to the ceiling 30 feet overhead and succeed on a DC 14 Dexterity check with thieves' tools, they may disarm this trap. If the trap is triggered, the character who triggered it must succeed on a DC 15 Dexterity saving throw or fall 200 feet and take 70 (20d6) bludgeoning damage in addition to being subjected to the green slime.

CIRCLE ELEVEN

This is a correct choice. This shaft leads to a sub-plane of your choosing, possibly the Sleepytime sub-plane described below. This circle is on the floor and has a thick yellow pus along its shaft. The pus bubbles in places and moves as if alive. At the end of a 200-foot shaft is a portal to the Sleepytime demiplane.

CIRCLE TWELVE

This is an incorrect choice. The wall of the shaft seems to have hard ivory ridges and is covered with purple ichor. Trapped within the magical stone and unable to writhe free is a **purple worm**. The worm gladly accepts any meals and shuts its maw only when a morsel or two present itself. Note, the purple worm cannot use its Tail Stinger in the tight shaft.

CIRCLE THIRTEEN

This is the final circle and an incorrect choice. The walls of the shaft are coated with a multitude of colored slime. The shaft is 200 feet tall, but 30 feet down is a portal that opens and deposits the characters 20 feet above the rolling slime sea to the south. The characters are thus likely fully submerged in the slime sea and face associated swimming and other difficulties.

SUB-PLANES

The Faceless Lord is very interested in running the rats (i.e., the characters) through his "toy" planes. He is not above using a booming telepathic voice to convince dimwitted characters to pick a shaft and attempt to find the riddle plates. The Faceless Lord also tends to ridicule anyone who retrieves a plate through the same omniscient voice. However, he is unlikely to confront anyone directly until the riddle is assembled and the obelisk opened.

The sub-planes are up to you to create, but it is suggested that you make these strange and wild places that the characters might not normally encounter. This option provides you with many avenues to explore; entirely new tangents to a campaign could start with adventures in these sub-planes. Alternatively, you may wish to forego the use of sub-planes and begin this encounter with the four riddle plates already in place. The plates weigh 50 pounds each and are made of stone.

The following are examples of sub-planes you may use. In each of these planes, the Faceless Lord appears as a different avatar. While the characters are in these sub-planes, time should not progress on their home plane to ensure that they are not trapped within the cube when the light of the blood moon passes. Also, once the characters retrieve the plates, they are all immediately teleported back through the hole into which they fell.

SLIME HOLE

In Slime Hole, the characters are dropped into the center of the foulest swamp in all the multiverse. Constant bubbles of methane gas seep up from below the muck to create gigantic bubbles that burst in riotous explosions. Depraved and wicked halflings inhabit the swamp and attempt to trick and lure the characters into danger. The Faceless Lord poses as the king of these halflings and uses the first plate as the back of his throne.

OGRE ROCKS

In Ogre Rocks, the characters appear on the side of a gigantic mountain. Under four suns, the characters must search for food and water in the rocky and uneven mountain chain populated by numerous giants and humanoids. The characters must journey to the only flat area, a gigantic amphitheater. Arriving in time for an eclipse of all four suns, a great concert begins with most of the vile populace in the audience. On stage, a group of ogres plays to the crowd with guttural cries and some sacrifices. The Faceless Lord poses as a large green ogre using the second plate as the back of his string bass.

ASTEROID

The characters find themselves popped into a deep tunnel within an unstable asteroid. The caverns flow in all three directions as gravity constantly shifts. The characters must avoid opening holes in the asteroid and being sucked out into the void. At the center of the asteroid, a city of encephalon gorgers cowers in fear from a gigantic beast that hunts them in the tunnels and passageways. The beast is the Faceless Lord, and the breastplate of his armor is the third plate.

SLEEPYTIME

The characters land softly in a field of poppies. Nearby sits the village of Sleepytime with its many faeries and joyous elves. Everyone is very, very happy in Sleepytime — until the block tower strikes the hour as the sun sets, that is. At this time, the poppy fields and babbling brooks turn to volcanic rock and rivers of molten lead. The sun quickly disappears, and the friendly inhabitants transform into undead and bloodthirsty demons. At sunrise, however, the clock tower tolls again and everything is once again "right" in Sleepytime. The fourth plate is actually the face of the clock on the clock tower. The Faceless Lord poses as the mayor of this happy village.

THE FOUR PLATES

Once all four plates are acquired, the endgame plays out. A plate fits only into its corresponding slot on the cube in the vault. Each plate originally had Abyssal writing. This vile writing has been marked through and replaced with an ancient Dwarvish dialect even older than that spoken in the "Siege of Orcus." Although someone may guess the answer to the riddle without all of the plates, the obelisk only opens once all four plates are returned.

With the plates assembled, someone who reads and writes Dwarvish has a moderate chance to decipher the ancient dialect. Magical means of interpretation are possible. The runes glow with a white light. They read:

PLATE ONE

> *Giant Killer am I!*
> *Some kill for me,*
> *Others wish to be as tough as me;*
> *I can make others thirst with envy.*

PLATE TWO

> *For some a tool,*
> *For others a barrier,*
> *I will survive past all that stands before me.*

PLATE THREE

> *I come in all colors, shapes, and sizes,*
> *From the smallest speck to the greatest mountain;*
> *I am an instrument of life and death.*

PLATE FOUR

> *I am silent and patient.*
> *You have tread upon me and I have surrounded you!*
> *Speak my name …*

The answer is "stone" or "rock." The obelisk unleashes a *lightning bolt* upon any character who verbalizes an incorrect answer. The character must make a DC 17 Dexterity saving throw. On a failure, they take 28 (8d6) lightning damage, or half as much on a success. A correct answer makes the obelisk unfold like a flower, with all four sides falling away slowly to reveal the demon's amulet.

The Abyssal writing beneath the Dwarvish riddle reads as follows: "May the Lord of Slime slumber … not take … amulet … beyond reach … freedom." This refers to the fact that anyone taking the amulet beyond the doorway frees the Faceless Lord from the magical wards of the vault and his divinely imposed obligation to protect it.

THE DEMON'S AMULET

The Faceless Lord's amulet is an artifact. It is a three-foot-wide crescent made of red gold. Spikes protrude all about it. At the apex of the crescent is the Faceless Lord's symbol. Anyone who directly touches the amulet to take possession of it and control the Faceless Lord must make a DC 18 Wisdom saving throw. Failure means that the character loses all hope and dies as his soul is sucked from his body and he or she collapses into a puddle of **green slime** (see **Appendix B**). Success allows the player to bargain with the Faceless Lord. A character may touch the amulet with a cloth or other object and ignore the saving throw, but he or she cannot command or strike a bargain with the Faceless Lord without making physical contact with the amulet. An elaborate ritual that is most likely beyond the characters' current knowledge and abilities is required to destroy the amulet (a potential reason why the characters must take the amulet to their benefactor).

If anyone standing on the island attempts to remove the amulet, the Faceless Lord communicates telepathically with the party. The words "YOU KNOW NOT WHAT YOU HAVE WROUGHT!" assault the minds of all of the party members, and the Faceless Lord reveals himself. If not, the Faceless Lord bides his time to see if the characters gain possession of the amulet.

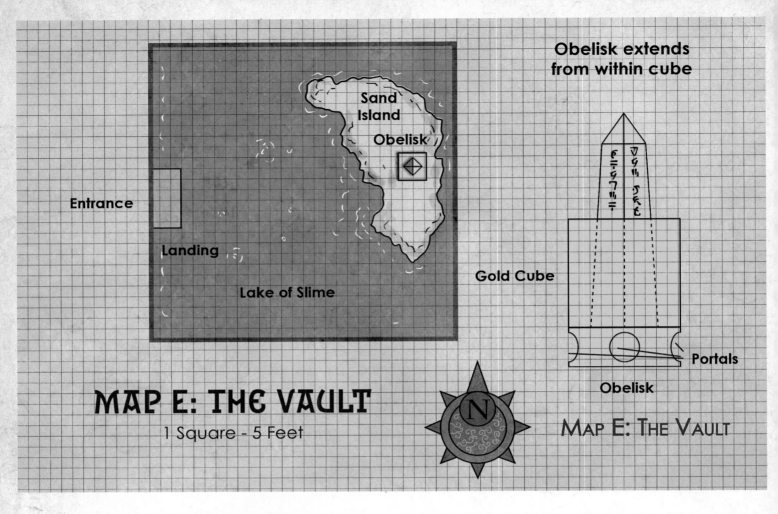

MAP E: THE VAULT
1 Square - 5 Feet

Sand Island

Obelisk

Entrance

Landing

Lake of Slime

Obelisk extends from within cube

Gold Cube

Portals

Obelisk

MAP E: THE VAULT

When he appears, the column of filth that is the Faceless Lord's avatar rises up behind the party in the slime ocean. The Faceless Lord does not immediately attack.

The Faceless Lord deeply desires the amulet, but Dwurfater's magic prevents him from leaving unless the amulet is removed. He attempts to use his influence and horrific presence to barter with the characters to remove the amulet for him. This is a situation in which the characters must deal with the demon or face destruction.

The Faceless Lord's bargain with the characters is simple: Take the amulet beyond the threshold of the vault in exchange for their lives. The Faceless Lord has no intention of keeping this bargain, however, and liquefies the characters as soon as he is free. If the characters take such a bargain, then they'll have to live with the obvious consequences. The Faceless Lord might also suggest that the bargain occur outside the vault, where both parties to the negotiation will be on even ground. The demon lord tries anything from threats to outrageous promises to get his amulet back.

To gain the upper hand, the characters should threaten not to remove the amulet. By the end of the night, the door to the vault will close and the Faceless Lord will have to wait a very long time before someone else successfully opens the vault. If the characters use this eventuality as leverage, the Faceless Lord is amenable to self-banishment for 100 years if the characters remove the amulet. The Faceless Lord agrees to such a bargain even if he does not get the amulet back. The Faceless Lord must keep this agreement, for once a demon pledges banishment he cannot break it — assuming that the characters can take possession of the amulet.

The characters may attempt to command the Faceless Lord. Each command after gaining possession (as described above) requires another DC 18 Wisdom saving throw, with the same deadly effects for failure. Such commands must be simple but can include self-banishment.

Again, how the bargain is made and what it consists of is up to you. Once the party leaves with the amulet and the Faceless Lord is either destroyed or banished, the adventure is effectively over.

If the characters foolishly try to kill the Faceless Lord, they are very, very likely to die. It should be assumed that the Faceless Lord immediately dispatches the characters. The only reason the characters are still alive is on the off chance one of them might take the amulet out of the vault. If that seems unlikely to happen and the characters don't figure out how to banish the fiend, the Faceless Lord likely consumes them. The statistics for the **Avatar of Jubilex** are included in **Appendix B**, in the event that the characters feel that combat is absolutely necessary and if you are willing to indulge them.

Jubilex, the Faceless Lord, Prince of Slime, is one of the most disgusting and loathsome of all demons. He takes the form of a mass of revolting liquid that is predominantly a swirl of brown, yellow, and purple. Various glaring red eyes are located throughout this liquid form.

Motivation: The Faceless Lord is a constant plotter, always devising a scheme to accomplish a task that will in turn help along another plot, and so on. Unfortunately for his followers, the Faceless Lord is apt to completely forget about a plot or to change his methods in the middle of a task. See above for the Faceless Lord's specific motivation in this adventure.

The Faceless Lord's entourage may be summoned at any time he is outside the vault. These vile slimes are dispersed in an area within 50 feet of the Faceless Lord. The entourage will not physically move to attack an enemy, but will take a strategic position to defend their lord. The entourage includes 1d2 **black puddings**, 1d4 **gelatinous cubes**, 1d4 **gray oozes**, and 1d6 **ochre jellies**.

EPILOGUE

You can conclude and continue the adventure in a number of ways. One way would be for the sponsoring church or benefactor to appear after the characters are victorious. Perhaps the church sent an army and is in the final stages of routing the remains of Lord Raob's force when the characters emerge from the vault. Sleeara and Lord Raob might be taken into custody, to return at some later date to exact their revenge. The church heavily rewards the characters and provides any necessary healing and resurrections.

Another approach to ending the adventure is if the bone devil, who was spying on the characters, learned of the characters' true mission. The bone devil's master hired a group to steal the amulet from the characters. If not already used, this group could be the Silver Eyes. The characters must contend with this group as they attempt to make their way back to civilization from the Devil's Finger. This approach may be too difficult for weary characters, however.

Alternatively, you could use the amulet as a means for the characters to garner the unwanted attention of a variety of unsavory beings. The Faceless Lord is perhaps banished, yet this does not stop him from sending his minions after the characters. Orcus may learn of the characters' success and send a number of followers after the characters as well. Another ending could be that goodly beings appear and demand the amulet for their safekeeping. In any event, many hearts in many places secretly covet the amulet, and this desire can be the start of attempts to seize it before the characters can return it to the church to be destroyed.

Now that the characters have the amulet, their trip back to civilization or another destination makes for an interesting continuation to this story. Dealing with the machinations of demons and being in possession of a great artifact is in the future. The heroes won the day on the Devil's Finger. They survived the chaotic maelstrom and defeated evil.

Yet evil is never defeated. It shall return once again another day …

APPENDIX A: NEW MAGIC

NEW SPELLS

GREEN WATER
1st-level transmutation

Casting Time: 1 action
Range: Touch
Components: V, S, M
Duration: Instantaneous
When you touch up to 10 gallons of water, it turns into green slime (see **Appendix B**).

MUCK
3rd-level conjuration

Casting Time: 1 action
Range: 100 feet
Components: V, S, M
Duration: 10 minutes
A patch of viscous, nearly indestructible, semi-sentient muck appears in a 20-foot square centered on a point you select within range. For the duration, this muck turns the ground in the area into difficult terrain. The muck may only be destroyed if it takes 20 cold damage or by a spell such as *wish*.

Creatures in the area when you cast the spell and those who enter the area or begin their turn there are grabbed by flailing pseudopods and must succeed on a Strength saving throw or be restrained by the sticky muck. A creature restrained by the muck can use its action to make a Strength check against your spell save DC. On a success, it frees itself.

When the spell ends, the conjured muck dries up, cracks, and blows away.

MUCUS MASK
4th-level conjuration

Casting Time: 1 action
Range: 40 feet
Components: V, S, M
Duration: 5 minutes
You hurl a glob of mucus at a creature within range. The mucus grows during flight. Make a ranged spell attack against the target. On a hit, the mucus engulfs the target's head, and the target takes 2d6 acid damage and is blinded, deafened, and unable to breathe. At the beginning of each of its subsequent turns, a target may use its action to make a Constitution saving throw. On a success, the mucus has been cleared from its eyes, ears, or mouth and one of the three conditions caused by the mucus mask is ended.

OOZE BOLT
3rd-level evocation

Casting Time: 1 action
Range: 30 ft.
Components: V, S
Duration: Instantaneous
You shoot a bolt of corrosive ooze at one creature you can see. Make a ranged spell attack against that creature. If it hits, the creature takes 6d4 acid damage immediately and an additional 4d4 acid damage at the end of each of its turns for the duration of the spell.

At Higher Levels. For each spell slot used higher than 3rd level, *ooze bolt* does an additional 2d4 acid damage on its initial hit.

PORTAL RUNE
5th-level conjuration

Casting Time: 1 action
Range: Touch
Components: V, S
Duration: Until dispelled
When you cast this spell, you touch a creature, and a portal key is tattooed on the target creature's flesh at a location of your choice. Such a portal key allows the target to open a specific inter-planar portal identified by the rune used. This portal key can be removed only with a wish, or similar spell or by destroying the flesh where the rune is inscribed. An unwilling target can resist the the effects of this spell by succeeding on a Wisdom saving throw.

ROT TO THE CORE
8th level enchantment

Casting Time: 1 action
Range: Touch
Components: V, S, M (a jar of toxic mushrooms)
Duration: Instantaneous
Make a melee spell attack on a creature you can reach. On a hit, the target takes 10d6 + 40 necrotic damage. If this damage reduces the target to 0 hit points, it is pulpified.

A pulpified creature's flesh and everything it is wearing and carrying, except magic items, are transformed to a bright orange pulp. The creature can be restored to life only by means of a *true resurrection* or a *wish* spell. Immediately after a target is pulpified, its body breaks open with liquid and spores spewing out of every orifice. These spores form a 20-foot-diameter cloud. Any creature except you caught in the spore cloud must succeed on a Constitution saving throw or take 2d6 necrotic damage and become diseased. The disease spores take root in its flesh, dealing another 1d6 necrotic damage each day as they grow until they are removed with *cure disease*.

SLIME BUCKET
5th-level conjuration

Casting Time: 1 action
Range: 150 ft.
Components: V, S
Duration: Instantaneous
You conjure a glob of heat-absorbing slime at a point you can see in the air. It then spreads and extends hairlike filaments downward throughout a 10-foot radius, 40-foot high cylinder. Each creature in the area takes 8d6 cold damage, or half damage with a successful Dexterity saving throw.

At Higher Levels. For each spell slot used higher than 5th level, the initial damage increases by 1d6.

SLIMEBALL
4th level evocation

Casting Time: 1 action
Range: 150 ft.
Components: V, S, M (a vial of acid)
Duration: Instantaneous
You shoot a ball of slime from your hand to a point you can see. The ball then explodes into a 20-foot-radius sphere. Each creature in the affected area must make a Dexterity saving throw. If the saving throw fails, the creature takes 6d6 acid damage immediately and 2d6 acid damage at the end of its next turn. On a successful save, a creature takes half damage immediately and 1d6 acid damage at the end of its next turn.

At Higher Levels. For each spell slot used higher than 4th level, *slimeball* does an additional 1d6 damage immediately. For each sorcery point you expend when casting the spell, the additional damage persists for an extra round. The maximum number of sorcery points that can be expended equals one-half the level of the spell slot used, rounded down.

New Magical Items

Boots of Haste

Wondrous item, very rare (requires attunement)

These boots have 3 charges. While wearing them, you can use a bonus action and expend 1 charge to cast *haste* on yourself. The effect lasts for 1 minute and does not require concentration. The boots regain 1d2 expended charges daily at dawn.

Cloak of Protection

Wondrous item, rarity varies (requires attunement)

While wearing this cloak, you gain a bonus to your AC and saving throws. The amount of the bonus depends on the cloak's rarity.

Cloak of…	Rarity	Bonus
Protection	uncommon	+1
Greater protection	rare	+2
Superior protection	very rare	+3

Liquor of Vomit

Potion, rare

This is a horrific brew. It has the consistency of mucus, the color of pus, and the odor of the dirtiest troglodyte in all of creation.

If you drink it,, you must make a DC 15 Constitution saving throw. On a failed save, you are cursed. While cursed, you wretch and vomit incessantly and have disadvantage on all Constitution saving throws and checks. Also, your alignment is changed to chaotic evil. The alteration is mental as well as moral, and you thoroughly enjoy your new outlook. Only a *remove curse* spell cast using a 5th level or higher spell slot (or a *wish* spell) may remove the curse.

Painting of Enlightenment

Wondrous item, rare

A *painting of enlightenment* is a magical work of art. The scene depicted in the painting appears to move, its motion dependent upon your position in relation to the painting. If you shuffle left to right, the particular scene is viewed in chronological sequence. If, however, you move right to left when beholding the painting, the scene plays out in reverse — horses appear to run backward, the sun sets in the east, and so on. A *painting of enlightenment* may depict any event, real or imagined, that the artist desires, though the detail of the scenes is restricted by the physical size of the canvas.

Staff of Sludge

Staff, very rare

This unusual staff is a favorite among the twisted followers of the Faceless Lord because of its ability to summon oozes. This long, wooden staff is knotted and twisted, and it seeps and pumps out a green ichor as if it were a living being. The staff has 3 charges and regains 1d3 expended charges daily at dawn. You can use an action to expend 1 charge from it to attempt to conjure forth an ooze by rolling on the table below. Yet there is a chance every time you use the staff that you will be reduced to a puddle of muck.

1d12	Summoned Ooze	
1–2	green slime (see Appendix B)	
3–5	gray ooze	
6–7	ochre jelly	
8–10	gelatinous cube	
11	black pudding	
12	You must succeed at a DC 12 Wisdom saving throw or be reduced to a puddle of green slime (see Appendix B). All of your nonmagical, non-stone possessions are immediately destroyed.	

Totem of the Gate

Wondrous item, legendary

A *totem of the gate* is a magical device that opens a portal identical to that created by the *gate* spell with the exceptions noted below. The totem is six inches long and looks like a chalk stick carved in the shape of a demon. To activate the totem, you draw the appropriate pentagram on a surface. The totem is a one-time use item. The portal is thereafter permanent and impervious to any magical attack (e.g. *dispel magic* and so forth). The only means of eliminating the *gate* is by breaking the *totem of the gate* in half, which destroys the magic and causes all creatures that have traversed the portal in either direction to disappear and reappear on their home plane.

Warning Cube

Wondrous item, rare

A *warning cube* is a six-inch silver cube with intricate runes covering its surface. When you hold the cube in your hand, it continuously detects a specific effect in a 30-foot radius. Many types of *warning cubes* exist, each one able to detect a different effect or type of object: animals, plants, traps and secret doors (similar to a *wand of secrets*), magic (similar to a *detect magic* spell), evil and good (similar to a *detect evil and good* spell), or poison and disease (similar to a *detect poison and disease* spell).

Once an effect is detected, the *warning cube* points in the direction of the detected object, and a *magic mouth* activates on the cube and shouts a specific phrase designated by the creator.

APPENDIX B: NEW MONSTERS

Allip

Medium undead, chaotic evil

Armor Class 11
Hit Points 33 (6d8 + 6)
Speed fly 30 ft.

STR	DEX	CON	INT	WIS	CHA
6 (–2)	13 (+1)	13 (+1)	11 (+0)	11 (+0)	16 (+3)

Skills Perception +3, Stealth +3
Senses darkvision 60 ft., passive Perception 13
Languages Common, Deep Speech
Challenge 2 (450 XP)

Babble. The allip incoherently mutters to itself, creating a hypnotic effect. All creatures within 30 ft. that aren't incapacitated must succeed on a DC 11 Wisdom saving throw. On a failed save, the creature becomes charmed for the duration. While charmed by this spell, the creature is incapacitated and has a speed of 0. The effect ends for an affected creature if it takes any damage or if someone else uses an action to shake the creature out of its stupor.

Madness. Anyone targeting an allip with a spell or effect that would make direct contact with its tortured mind must succeed on a DC 11 Wisdom saving throw or take 7 (2d6) psychic damage.

Actions

Touch of Insanity. *Melee Weapon Attack:* +3 to hit, reach 5 ft., one target. *Hit:* 8 (2d6 + 1) psychic damage.

Avatar of Jubilex

Huge fiend (demon), chaotic evil

Armor Class 23
Hit Points 580 (40d12 + 320)
Speed 30 ft., climb 30 ft., fly 40 ft., swim 30 ft.

STR	DEX	CON	INT	WIS	CHA
23 (+6)	20 (+5)	26 (+8)	27 (+8)	24 (+7)	19 (+4)

Skills Arcana +17, Deception +22, History +17, Perception +16, Religion +17
Damage Resistances cold, damage from spells, fire, lightning, piercing
Damage Immunities acid, necrotic, poison; bludgeoning, piercing, and slashing from nonmagical attacks
Condition Immunities charmed, exhaustion, frightened, poisoned, prone
Senses truesight 120 ft., passive Perception 26
Languages telepathy 240 ft.
Challenge 30 (155,000 XP)

Acid Form. The avatar of Jubilex can move through a space as narrow as 1 inch wide without squeezing. A creature that touches the avatar of Jubilex or hits it with a melee attack while within 5 feet of it must succeed on a DC 20 Constitution saving throw or take 15 (6d4) acid damage immediately and at the end of its next turn. In addition, the avatar of Jubilex can enter a hostile creature's space and stop there. The first time it enters a creature's space on a turn, that creature takes 28 (8d6) acid damage.

Spider Climb. The avatar of Jubilex can climb difficult surfaces, including upside down on ceilings, without needing to make an ability check.

Innate Spellcasting. The avatar of Jubilex's innate spellcasting ability is Intelligence (spell save DC 25, +17 to hit with spell attacks). The avatar of Jubilex can innately cast the following spells, requiring no material components:

At will: *darkness, fear*
5/day each: *contagion, dispel magic* (6th level slot), *invisibility, telekinesis*
3/day each: *dominate monster, gate, harm, hold monster* (7th level slot)

Legendary Resistance (3/day). If the avatar of Jubilex fails a saving throw, it can choose to succeed instead.

Magic Weapons. The avatar of Jubilex's weapon attacks are magical.

Actions

Multiattack. The avatar of Jubilex makes three attacks, only one of which may be a Toxic Spray attack or a Whelm attack.

Slam. *Melee Weapon Attack:* +15 to hit, reach 10 ft., one target. *Hit:* 28 (4d10 + 6) bludgeoning damage. The target must succeed on a DC 20 Constitution saving throw or take 15 (6d4) acid damage immediately and at the end of its next turn.

Toxic Spray. The avatar of Jubilex sprays poisonous slime in a 30-foot radius circle around it. Each non-ooze creature in that area must make a DC 20 Constitution saving throw, taking 35 (10d6) poison damage on a failed save, or half as much damage on a successful one. Targets who fail their save are poisoned until the end of the avatar of Jubilex's next turn.

Whelm. Each creature in the avatar of Jubilex's space must make a DC 20 Strength saving throw. On a failure, a target takes 28 (8d6) acid damage. If it is Large or smaller, it is also grappled (escape DC 20). Until this grapple ends, the target is restrained and unable to breathe. If the saving throw is successful, the target is pushed out of the avatar of Jubilex's space.

The avatar of Jubilex can grapple one Large creature or up to two Medium or smaller creatures at one time. At the start of each of the avatar of Jubilex's turns, each target grappled by it takes 28 (8d6) acid damage. A creature within 5 feet of the avatar of Jubilex can pull a creature or object out of it by taking an action to make a DC 20 Strength check and succeeding.

Legendary Actions

The avatar of Jubilex can take 3 legendary actions, choosing from the options below. Only one legendary action option can be used at a time and only at the end of another creature's turn. The avatar of Jubilex regains spent legendary actions at the start of its turn.

Cast a Spell (costs 3 actions). The avatar of Jubilex innately casts one of its spells.

Slam. The avatar of Jubilex makes one Slam attack.

Toxic Spray (costs 2 actions). The avatar of Jubilex makes one Toxic Spray attack

Summon Ooze (costs 2 actions). The avatar of Jubilex calls forth an ooze servant. An ooze creature of challenge rating 6 or lower appears in an unoccupied space within 20 feet of it. The creature is friendly to the avatar of Jubilex. Roll initiative for the creature, which has its own turns. It obeys any verbal or telepathic commands that the avatar of Jubilex issues to it.

BURGLAR

Medium humanoid (any), any alignment

Armor Class 15 (leather armor)
Hit Points 52 (8d8 + 16)
Speed 30 ft.

STR	DEX	CON	INT	WIS	CHA
13 (+1)	18 (+4)	15 (+2)	12 (+1)	14 (+2)	10 (+0).

Saving Throws Dex +7, Int +4
Skills Acrobatic +7, Athletics +4, Perception +5, Sleight of Hand +7, Stealth +7
Senses passive Perception 15
Languages Thieves' cant plus any two languages
Challenge 5 (1,800 XP)

Cunning Action. The burglar can use a bonus action on its turn to take the Dash, Disengage, Hide, or Use an Object action.
Evasion. When the burglar is subjected to an effect that allows it to make a Dexterity saving throw to take only half damage, it instead takes no damage if the saving throw is successful, and only half damage if the roll is a failure.
Sneak Attack. Once per turn, the burglar can deal an extra 14 (4d6) damage to one creature it hits with an attack if it has advantage on the attack roll. The attack must use a finesse or ranged weapon. The burglar doesn't need advantage on the attack roll if another enemy of the target is within 5 feet of it, that enemy isn't incapacitated, and the burglar doesn't have disadvantage on the attack roll.

ACTIONS

Multiattack. The burglar can make two attacks with either its Shortsword, its Dagger, or its Light Crossbow.
Shortsword. Melee Weapon Attack: +7 to hit, reach 5 ft., one target. *Hit:* 7 (1d6 + 4) piercing damage.
Dagger. Melee or Ranged Weapon Attack: +7 to hit, reach 5 ft. or range 20/60 ft., one target. *Hit:* 6 (1d4 + 4) piercing damage.
Light Crossbow. Ranged Weapon Attack: +7 to hit, range 80/320 ft., one target. *Hit:* 8 (1d8 + 4) piercing damage.

CAPTAIN

Medium humanoid (any race), any alignment

Armor Class 18 (chain mail and shield)
Hit Points 65 (10d8+20)
Speed 30 ft.

STR	DEX	CON	INT	WIS	CHA
18 (+4)	10 (+0)	15 (+2)	12 (+1)	12 (+1)	16 (+3)

Saving Throws Str +6, Con +4
Skills Athletics +6, Perception +5, Intimidation +7
Senses passive Perception 15
Languages Common, Dwarvish
Challenge 4 (1,100 XP)

Brave. The captain has advantage on all saving throws against fear.
Leadership (recharges after a short or long rest). For 1 minute, the captain can utter a special command or warning whenever a nonhostile creature that it can see within 30 feet of it makes an attack roll or a saving throw. The creature can add a d4 to its roll provided it can hear and understand the captain. A creature can benefit from only one Leadership die at a time. This effect ends if the captain is incapacitated.

ACTIONS

Multiattack. The captain makes three melee attacks.
Longsword. Melee Weapon Attack: +6 to hit, reach 5 ft., one target. *Hit:* 8 (1d8 + 4) slashing damage, or 9 (1d10 + 4) if used with two hands.
Heavy Crossbow. Ranged Weapon Attack: +2 to hit, range 100/400, one target. *Hit:* 5 (1d10) piercing damage.

COMMANDER

Medium humanoid (any race), any alignment

Armor Class 19 (splint, shield)
Hit Points 110 (17d8+34)
Speed 30 ft.

STR	DEX	CON	INT	WIS	CHA
19 (+4)	12 (+1)	14 (+2)	13 (+1)	14 (+2)	12 (+1)

Saving Throws Str +7, Con +5
Skills Animal Handling +5, Athletics +7, Insight +5, Perception +5
Senses passive Perception 15
Languages Common, and one other
Challenge 5 (1,800 XP)

Indomitable (1/day). The commander rerolls a failed saving throw.
Second Wind (recharges after a short or long rest). As a bonus action, the commander can regain 10 hit points.
Leadership (recharges after a short or long rest). For 1 minute, the commander can utter a special command or warning whenever a nonhostile creature that it can see within 30 feet of it makes an attack roll or a saving throw. The creature can add a d4 to its roll provided it can hear and understand the commander. A creature can benefit from only one Leadership die at a time. This effect ends if the commander is incapacitated.

ACTIONS

Multiattack. The commander makes three melee attacks.
Longsword. Melee Weapon Attack: +7 to hit, reach 5 ft., one target. *Hit:* 8 (1d8 + 4) slashing damage, or 9 (1d10 + 4) slashing damage if used with two hands.
Heavy Crossbow. Ranged Weapon Attack: +4 to hit, range 100/400, one target. *Hit:* 6 (1d10 + 1) piercing damage.

CORRUPTED

Medium humanoid, chaotic evil

Armor Class 15
Hit Points 52 (8d8 + 16)
Speed 30 ft.

STR	DEX	CON	INT	WIS	CHA
14 (+2)	10 (+0)	15 (+2)	3 (–4)	5 (–3)	5 (–3)

Damage Resistances bludgeoning, cold, fire
Damage Immunities acid
Condition Immunities charmed, exhaustion, poisoned
Senses darkvision 60 ft., passive Perception 7
Languages —

Challenge 3 (700 XP)

Regeneration. The corrupted regains 5 hit points at the start of its turn if it has at least 1 hit point. If the corrupted takes radiant damage, this trait doesn't function at the start of the corrupted's next turn.
Acid Form. A creature that touches the corrupted or hits it with a melee attack while within 5 feet of it must succeed on a DC 12 Constitution saving throw or take 5 (2d4) acid damage immediately and at the end of its next turn. When it dies, a corrupted also turns into a 5 foot pool of acid.

ACTIONS

Axe. Melee Weapon Attack: +4 to hit, reach 5 ft., one target. *Hit:* 7 (1d10 + 2) slashing damage.
Slam. Melee Weapon Attack: +4 to hit, reach 5 ft., one target. *Hit:* 5 (1d6 + 2) bludgeoning damage. The target must succeed on a DC 12 Constitution saving throw or take 5 (2d4) acid damage immediately and another 5 (2d4) acid damage at the end of its next turn.

Dark Custodian
Medium undead, chaotic evil

Armor Class 18
Hit Points 135 (18d8 + 54)
Speed 0 ft., fly 40 ft. (hover)

STR	DEX	CON	INT	WIS	CHA
11 (+0)	15 (+2)	16 (+3)	17 (+3)	20 (+5)	12 (+1)

Saving Throws Con +8, Int +8, Wis +10
Skills Arcana +8, History +8, Perception +10, Religion +8, Stealth +12
Damage Resistances acid, fire, lightning
Damage Immunities cold, necrotic, poison; bludgeoning, piercing, and slashing from nonmagical attacks
Condition Immunities charmed, exhaustion, frightened, grappled, paralyzed, petrified, poisoned, prone, restrained
Senses truesight 50 ft., passive Perception 20
Languages Common plus up to five other languages
Challenge 16 (15,000 XP)

Directed Hatred. The dark custodian has advantage on all attacks against one creature type chosen at the time the dark custodian comes into being.

Ethereal Sight. The dark custodian can see 60 ft. into the Ethereal Plane when he is on the Material Plane, and vice versa.

Incorporeal Movement. The dark custodian can move through other creatures and objects as if they were difficult terrain. It takes 5 (1d10) force damage if it ends its turn inside an object.

Turn Resistance. The dark custodian has advantage on saving throws against any effect that turns undead.

Spellcasting. The dark custodian is a 14th-level spellcaster. Its spellcasting ability is Wisdom (spell save DC 18, +10 to hit with spell attacks). It requires no material components to cast its spells. The dark custodian has the following cleric spells prepared:
Cantrips (at will): *resistance, sacred flame, thaumaturgy*
1st level (4 slots): *bane, command, sanctuary*
2nd level (3 slots): *blindness/deafness, hold person, silence,*
3rd level (3 slots): *bestow curse, dispel magic*
4th level (3 slots): *death ward, stone shape*
5th level (2 slots): *flame strike, insect plague*
6th level (1 slot): *harm*
7th level (1 slot): *fire storm*

Actions

Multiattack. The dark custodian makes two attacks, only one of which may be a Soul Drain attack.

Icy Touch. *Melee Weapon Attack:* +10 to hit, reach 5 ft., one target. *Hit:* 14 (2d8 + 5) cold damage and the target is grappled (escape DC 16). Until the grapple ends, the target is restrained and has disadvantage on Strength checks and Strength saving throws, and the dark custodian can't grapple another target.

Etherealness. The dark custodian enters the Ethereal Plane from the Material Plane, or vice versa. It is visible on the Material Plane while he is in the Border Ethereal, and vice versa, yet it can't affect or be affected by anything on the other plane. Any creature grappled by the dark custodian is transported with it. If a grappled creature breaks the grapple while in the Ethereal Plane, it returns to the Material Plane and appears in an unoccupied space within 5 feet of the dark custodian.

Soul Drain. The dark custodian drains the life essence of one creature it has grappled. The creature takes 23 (5d6 + 6) necrotic damage and its hit point maximum is reduced by the amount of necrotic damage taken. The dark custodian regains hit points equal to that amount. The reduction lasts until the creature finishes a long rest. The creature dies if this effect reduces its hit point maximum to 0. A humanoid slain in this way rises the following night as a specter spawn under the dark custodian's control.

Legendary Actions

The dark custodian can take 3 legendary actions, choosing from the options below. Only one legendary action option can be used at a time and only at the end of another creature's turn. The dark custodian regains spent legendary actions at the start of its turn.
Icy Touch. The dark custodian makes one Icy Touch attack.
Summon Undead (costs 2 actions). The dark custodian calls forth an undead servant. An undead creature of challenge rating 5 or lower appears in an unoccupied space within 10 feet of it. The creature is friendly to the dark custodian. Roll initiative for the creature, which has its own turns. It obeys any verbal commands that the dark custodian issues to it.
Madness of the Grave (costs 2 actions). The dark custodian focuses all of the rage and frustration of its unending unlife on one creature it can see within 20 feet of it. The target must succeed on a DC 18 Wisdom saving throw against this magic or take 11 (2d10) psychic damage and become maddened for 1 minute. A maddened target uses its action to make a melee attack against a randomly determined creature within its reach. If no creatures are within its reach, it screams in frustration and does nothing this turn. The maddened target can repeat the saving throw at the end of each of its turns, ending the effect on itself on a success. If a target's saving throw is successful or the effect ends for it, the target is immune to the dark custodian's Madness of the Grave for the next 24 hours.
Cast a Spell (costs 2 actions). The dark custodian casts a spell from its list of prepared spells, using a spell slot as normal.

Death Mage (Necromancer)
Medium humanoid (any), any alignment

Armor Class 12 (15 with *mage armor*)
Hit Points 66 (12d8+12)
Speed 30 ft.

STR	DEX	CON	INT	WIS	CHA
9 (−1)	14 (+2)	12 (+1)	17 (+3)	12 (+1)	11 (+0)

Saving Throws Int +7, Wis +5
Skills Arcana +7, History +7
Senses passive Perception 11
Languages Any four languages
Challenge 9 (5,000 XP)

Spellcasting. The deathmage is a 12th-level spellcaster. Its spellcasting ability is Intelligence (spell save DC 15, +7 to hit with spell attacks). It has the following wizard spells prepared:
Cantrips (at will): *chill touch, dancing lights, mage hand, mending*
1st level (4 slots): *false life, mage armor, shield*
2nd level (3 slots): *blindness/deafness, ray of enfeeblement, web*
3rd level (3 slots): *animate dead, bestow curse, vampiric touch*
4th level (3 slots): *blight, dimension door, stoneskin*
5th level (2 slots): *cloudkill, dominate person*
6th level (1 slots): *circle of death*

Actions

Grim Harvest. When deathmage kills a creature that is neither a construct nor undead with a spell of 1st level or higher, the deathmage regains hit points equal to twice the spell's level, or three times if it is a necromancy spell.

Quarterstaff. *Melee Weapon Attack:* +1 to hit, reach 5 ft., one target. *Hit:* 2 (1d6 − 1) bludgeoning damage, or 3 (1d8 − 1) bludgeoning damage if used with two hands.

ENCEPHALON GORGER
Medium aberration, chaotic evil

Armor Class 16 (natural armor)
Hit Points 71 (11d8 + 22)
Speed 30 ft.

STR	DEX	CON	INT	WIS	CHA
12 (+1)	16 (+3)	14 (+2)	20 (+5)	15 (+2)	15 (+2)

Skills Perception +5, Stealth +6
Senses darkvision 60 ft., passive Perception 15
Languages Common, Deep Speech, telepathy 120 ft.
Challenge 7 (2,900 XP)

Alien Mind. Encephalon gorgers can maintain concentration on 3 simultaneous spell effects.

Mindsense. The encephalon gorger is aware of the presence of creatures within 300 feet of it that have an Intelligence of 3 or higher. It knows the relative distance and direction of each creature, as well as the creature's approximate Intelligence score (within 3 points). Creatures under the effects of magic that protects the mind cannot be detected by the encephalon gorger.

Mind Screen. The mind of an encephalon gorger is an alien and dangerous place. Should a creature attempt to scan the mind or read the thoughts of an encephalon gorger (with *detect thoughts*, telepathy, or the like), it must succeed on a DC 15 Intelligence saving throw or be driven insane, gaining a flaw from the Indefinite Madness table (see the SRD). On a successful save, the creature is confused for 1 minute (as the *confusion* spell).

ACTIONS

Multiattack. The encephalon gorger makes two attacks with its Claws and uses Mindfeed if it has a creature grappled.

Claws. *Melee Weapon Attack:* +6 to hit, reach 5 ft., one target. *Hit:* 10 (2d6 + 3) slashing damage If the target is Medium or smaller, it is grappled (escape DC 16). Until this grapple ends, the target is restrained, and the encephalon gorger can only use its Mindfeed on the grappled creature and has advantage on attack rolls to do so.

Mindfeed. *Melee Weapon Attack:* +6 to hit, reach 5 ft., one creature that is grappled by the encephalon gorger. *Hit:* 7 (1d8 + 3) piercing damage, and the target must succeed on a DC 15 Intelligence saving throw, or take 33 (6d10) psychic damage, and the target's Intelligence score is reduced by 1d4. The target dies if this reduces its Intelligence to 0. Otherwise, the reduction lasts until the target finishes a long rest.

Adrenal Surge (2/day). The encephalon gorger surges with adrenaline until the end of its turn. While under this effect, it gains a +2 bonus to its AC, it has advantage on Dexterity saving throws, and it gains an additional action on its turn (as the *haste* spell).

GREEN SLIME

Green slime is corrosive, slick, and adhesive, sticking to anything it comes into contact with. Metal, flesh, organic material is especially vulnerable to the corrosive properties of the slime. It is often found in warm, humid caverns and ruins, and will be noticeable as it clings to ceilings, walls, and covers floors, usually in five-foot squares.

Green slime can detect movement within 30 feet and will drop on unsuspecting victims when they are below it; it is unable to move so much depends on unwitting prey. If a creature is aware of the presence of the slime, they can attempt to avoid the hazard by succeeding on a DC 10 Dexterity saving throw.

The green slime secretes acid and does 5 (1d10) acid damage to any creature it comes into contact with. This damage continues on each of the creature's turns until it uses an action to remove or destroy the slime. Much like its more evolved ooze relatives, the green slime is doubly caustic to nonmagical wood and metal, doing 11 (2d10) acid damage against objects of these types.

Green slime is vulnerable to and will be destroyed by fire, cold, radiant damage, sunlight or any disease curing magic.

DEMONVESSEL
Medium undead, chaotic evil

Armor Class 16 (natural armor)
Hit Points 97 (13d8 + 39)
Speed 30 ft.

STR	DEX	CON	INT	WIS	CHA
16 (+3)	13 (+1)	17 (+3)	14 (+2)	16 (+3)	10 (+0)

Skills Deception +3, Perception +6, Stealth +4
Damage Resistances cold, fire, lightning; bludgeoning, piercing, and slashing from nonmagical attacks
Damage Immunities poison
Condition Immunities charmed, paralyzed, petrified, poisoned
Senses darkvision 60 ft., passive Perception 16
Languages Abyssal, Common
Challenge 7 (2,900 XP)

Fear Aura. Any creature hostile to the demonvessel that starts its turn within 20 feet of the demonvessel must make a DC 15 Wisdom saving throw, unless the demonvessel is incapacitated. On a failed save, the creature is frightened until the start of its next turn. If a creature's saving throw is successful, the creature is immune to the demonvessel's Fear Aura for the next 24 hours.

Magic Resistance. The demonvessel has advantage on saving throws against spells and other magical effects.

ACTIONS

Multiattack. The demonvessel makes three Claw attacks.
Claw. *Melee Weapon Attack:* +6 to hit, reach 5 ft., one target. *Hit:* 8 (1d10 + 3) slashing damage plus 9 (2d8) cold damage.

IMBO THE UNDYING

Medium humanoid (dwarf), chaotic evil

Armor Class 20 (*+1 adamantine breastplate*, shield)
Hit Points 131 (16d8 + 64)
Speed 40 ft.

STR	DEX	CON	INT	WIS	CHA
19 (+4)	15 (+2)	18 (+4)	16 (+3)	16 (+3)	15 (+2)

Saving Throws Str +8, Dex +6, Con +8, Int +7
Skills Acrobatics +10, Athletics +8, Deception +10, Perception +11, Sleight of Hand +6, Stealth +10
Senses passive Perception 21
Languages Common, Dwarvish, thieves' cant
Challenge 11 (7,200 XP)

***Action Surge* (recharges after a short or long rest).** On his turn, Imbo the Undying can take one additional action on top of his regular action and a possible bonus action.

Cunning Action. Imbo the Undying can take a bonus action on each of his turns in combat. The action can only be used to take the following actions: Dash, Disengage, Hide, Use an Object, make a Dexterity (Sleight of Hand) check, or use thieves' tools to disarm a trap or open a lock.

Defense. While Imbo the Undying is wearing armor, he gains a +1 bonus to AC (included above).

Evasion. When Imbo the Undying is subjected to an effect that allows him to make a Dexterity saving throw to take only half damage, he instead takes no damage if he succeeds on the saving throw, and only half damage if he fails.

Immune to Critical Hits. All critical hits against Imbo the Undying become normal hits because of his adamantine breastplate.

Reckless Attack. When Imbo the Undying makes his first attack on his turn, he can decide to attack recklessly. Doing so gives him advantage on melee weapon attack rolls using Strength during this turn, but attack rolls against him have advantage until his next turn.

Sneak Attack. Once per turn, if Imbo the Undying deals an extra 4d6 damage to one creature he hits with an attack if he has advantage on the attack roll. He does not need advantage on the attack roll if another enemy of the target is within 5 feet of it, that enemy isn't incapacitated, and Imbo the Undying does not have disadvantage on the attack roll.

Special Equipment. Imbo the Undying possesses *gauntlets of ogre power*, *boots of speed*, and an *ioun stone of leadership*.

Uncanny Dodge. When an attacker that he can see hits Imbo the Undying with an attack, he can use his reaction to halve the attack's damage against him.

ACTIONS

Multiattack. Imbo the Undying makes two weapon attacks.

+2 Dwarven Thrower. *Melee Weapon Attack*: +10 to hit, range 20/60 ft., one target. *Hit*: 15 (2d8 + 6) bludgeoning damage.

+1 Battleaxe. *Melee Weapon Attack*: +9 to hit, reach 5 ft., one target. *Hit*: 9 (1d8 + 5) slashing damage.

BONUS ACTIONS

***Rage* (4/day).** Imbo the Undying can enter a rage. While raging, he has advantage on Strength checks and Strength saving throws. When he makes a melee weapon attack using Strength, he gains a +2 bonus to the damage roll. He has resistance to bludgeoning, piercing, and slashing damage. This rage lasts for 1 minute. It ends early if Imbo the Undying is knocked unconscious or if his turn ends and he hasn't attacked a hostile creature since his last turn or taken damage since then. He can also end his rage on his turn as a bonus action.

***Second Wind* (recharges after a short or long rest).** Imbo the Undying regains 1d10 + 2 hit points.

KILLER

Medium humanoid (any race), any alignment

Armor Class 15 (studded leather)
Hit Points 38 (7d8 + 7)
Speed 30 ft.

STR	DEX	CON	INT	WIS	CHA
12 (+1)	16 (+3)	12 (+1)	13 (+1)	14 (+2)	13 (+1)

Saving Throws Dex +6, Int +4
Skills Athletics +4, Acrobatics +9, Deception +4, Perception +4, Stealth +9
Senses passive Perception 14
Languages Thieves' cant plus any two languages
Challenge 5 (1,800 XP)

Assassinate. During its first turn, the killer has advantage on attack rolls against any creature that hasn't yet acted in the combat. Any hit the killer scores against a surprised creature counts as a critical hit.

Cunning Action. On each of its turns, the killer can use a bonus action to take the Dash, Disengage, or Hide action.

***Sneak Attack* (1/turn).** Once per turn, the killer deals an extra 17 (5d6) damage when it hits a target with a weapon attack and has advantage on the attack roll, or when the target is within 5 feet of an ally of the killer that isn't incapacitated and the killer doesn't have disadvantage on the attack roll.

ACTIONS

Multiattack. The killer makes two Dagger or two Shortsword attacks.

Dagger. *Melee or Ranged Weapon Attack:* +6 to hit, reach 5 ft. or range 20/60 ft., one target. *Hit:* 5 (1d4 + 3) piercing damage.

Shortsword. *Melee Weapon Attack:* +6 to hit, reach 5 ft., one target. *Hit:* 6 (1d6 + 3) piercing damage.

LIVESTONE

Large ooze (fungus), unaligned

Armor Class 10
Hit Points 168 (16d10 + 80)
Speed 20 ft.

STR	DEX	CON	INT	WIS	CHA
20 (+5)	10 (+0)	20 (+5)	2 (−4)	1 (−5)	1 (−5)

Damage Immunities acid, cold, fire, poison
Condition Immunities blinded, charmed, deafened, exhaustion, frightened, poisoned, prone
Senses blindsight 60 ft. (blind beyond this radius), passive Perception 5
Languages —
Challenge 5 (1,800 XP)

False Appearance. While the livestone is solidified and remains motionless, it is indistinguishable from a typical stone.
Stone Camouflage. The livestone has advantage on Dexterity (Stealth) checks made to hide in rocky terrain.

ACTIONS

Multiattack. The livestone makes two attacks with its pseudopod.
Pseudopod. *Melee Weapon Attack:* +8 to hit, reach 5 ft., one target. *Hit:* 14 (2d8 + 5) bludgeoning damage. If the target is Medium or smaller, it is grappled (escape DC 15) and restrained until the grapple ends. The livestone can grapple two targets.
Engulf. The livestone engulfs a Medium or smaller creature grappled by it. The engulfed target is blinded, restrained, and unable to breathe, and it must succeed on a DC 15 Constitution saving throw at the start of each of the livestone's turns or take 14 (2d8 + 5) bludgeoning damage. If the livestone moves, the engulfed target moves with it. The livestone can have only one creature engulfed at a time.

REACTIONS

Solidify. As a reaction, the livestone can solidify all or part of itself into material with the same consistency of solid rock. The livestone adds 4 to its AC against one melee attack that would hit it. The livestone does not have to see the attack or be wielding a melee weapon to use this ability. A livestone cannot take attack or move actions if its entire form is solidified.

MUSTARD JELLY

Large ooze, unaligned

Armor Class 14 (natural armor)
Hit Points 136 (13d10 + 65)
Speed 30 ft.

STR	DEX	CON	INT	WIS	CHA
15 (+2)	10 (+0)	21 (+5)	10 (+0)	10 (+0)	10 (+0)

Skills Perception +4, Stealth +4
Damage Resistance cold
Damage Immunities force, lightning, poison
Condition Immunities blinded, charmed, deafened, exhaustion, frightened, poisoned
Senses blindsight 60 ft. (blind beyond this radius), passive Perception 14
Languages —
Challenge 6 (2,300 XP)

Amorphous. The jelly can move through a space as narrow as 1 inch wide without squeezing.
Energy Absorption. A mustard jelly is immune to force and lightning damage. If the jelly would have taken force or lightning damage, it is instead healed for the same amount it would have taken in damage.
Magic Weapons. The jelly's attacks are magical.
Spider Climb. The jelly can climb difficult surfaces, including upside down on ceilings, without needing to make an ability check.
Poison Aura. At the start of each of the jelly's turns, each creature within 10 feet of it takes 10 (3d6) poison damage. A creature that touches the jelly or hits it with a melee attack while within 5 feet of it takes 10 (3d6) poison damage.

ACTIONS

Pseudopod. *Melee Weapon Attack:* +5 to hit, reach 5 ft., one target. *Hit:* 12 (3d6 + 2) bludgeoning damage and 10 (3d6) acid damage.

PREACHER

Medium humanoid (any race), any alignment

Armor Class 16 (chain shirt, shield)
Hit Points 78 (12d8 + 24)
Speed 30 ft.

STR	DEX	CON	INT	WIS	CHA
16 (+3)	12 (+1)	14 (+2)	13 (+1)	20 (+5)	17 (+3)

Saving Throws Con +5, Wis +8
Skills History +4, Performance +6, Persuasion +9, Religion +4
Senses passive Perception 15
Languages any three languages
Challenge 8 (3,900 XP)

Spellcasting. The preacher is a 10th-level spellcaster. Its spellcasting ability is Wisdom (spell save DC 16, +8 to hit with spell attacks). The preacher has the following cleric spells prepared:

Cantrips (at will): *guidance, light, resistance, sacred flame, thaumaturgy*
1st level (4 slots): *bane, bless, command, cure wounds, inflict wounds*
2nd level (3 slots): *aid, hold person, spiritual weapon*
3rd level (3 slots): *beacon of hope, mass healing word, tongues*
4th level (3 slots): *freedom of movement, locate creature*
5th level (2 slots): *flame strike, geas*

Unshakeable Faith. The preacher has advantage on Wisdom and Charisma saving throws.

ACTIONS

Multiattack. The preacher uses its Speech and makes three melee attacks.

Morningstar. *Melee Weapon Attack:* +6 to hit, reach 5 ft., one target. *Hit:* 7 (1d8 + 3) piercing damage.

Speech. The preacher makes one of the following speeches; it can't use the same speech two rounds in a row:

Condemning Speech. The preacher speaks words of condemnation at one target within 30 feet of it. The target must make a DC 16 Wisdom saving throw. On a failure, the target takes 28 (8d6) thunder damage and is frightened for 1 minute. On a success, the target takes half the damage and isn't frightened. A frightened creature can repeat the saving throw at the end of each of its turns, ending the effect on itself on a success. If the creature's saving throw is successful or the effect ends for it, the creature is immune to the preacher's Condemning Speech for the next 24 hours.

Inspiring Speech. The preacher targets up to three creatures it can see within 30 feet of it and speaks words of inspiration. Each target has advantage on its next attack roll, saving throw, or ability check.

Swaying Speech. The preacher speaks persuasively to one target within 30 feet of it. The target must make a DC 16 Wisdom saving throw. On a failure, the target takes 28 (8d6) psychic damage and is charmed for 1 minute. On a success, the target takes half the damage and isn't charmed. A charmed creature can repeat the saving throw at the end of each of its turns, ending the effect on itself on a success. If a creature's saving throw is successful or the effect ends for it, the creature is immune to the preacher's Swaying Speech for the next 24 hours.

PRIEST OF ORCUS

Medium humanoid (human), chaotic evil

Armor Class 18 (chainmail, shield)
Hit Points 60 (11d8 + 11)
Speed 30 ft.

STR	DEX	CON	INT	WIS	CHA
14 (+2)	11 (+0)	13 (+1)	10 (+0)	18 (+4)	14 (+2)

Saving Throws Con +4, Wis +7
Skills History +3, Investigation +3, Medicine +7, Religion +3
Senses truesight 120 ft., passive Perception 14
Languages Abyssal, Common
Challenge 6 (2,300 XP)

Abyssal Blessing of Orcus. The priest of Orcus gains 15 temporary hit points when it reduces a hostile creature that is not undead to 0 hit points.

Deadsight. The most blessed of Orcus are gifted with truesight.

Unholy Strike. Once on each of the priest's turns when it hits a creature with a weapon attack, the priest can cause the attack to deal an extra 13 (3d8) necrotic damage to the target.

Unholy Weapon. Orcus bolsters his follower's strikes in battle, imbuing their weapons with the ability to paralyze a foe (included in the attack). In the hands of any but a true follower of Orcus, an unholy weapon loses its power to paralyze a foe.

Spellcasting. The priest of Orcus is an 8th-level spellcaster. Its spellcasting ability is Wisdom (spell save DC 15, +7 to hit with spell attacks). It has the following cleric spells prepared:

Cantrips (at will): *chill touch, guidance, resistance, thaumaturgy*
1st level (4 slots): *bane, bless, cure wounds, detect magic, false life, inflict wounds*
2nd level (3 slots): *enhance ability, hold person, silence*
3rd level (3 slots): *animate dead, bestow curse, dispel magic*
4th level (2 slots): *blight, guardian of faith*

ACTIONS

+1 Unholy Mace. *Melee Weapon Attack:* +6 to hit, reach 5 ft., one target. *Hit:* 9 (1d8 + 3) bludgeoning damage. If the target is a creature other than an elf or undead, it must succeed on a DC 10 Constitution saving throw or be paralyzed for 1 minute. The target can repeat the saving throw at the end of each of its turns, ending the effect on itself on a success.

Caress of Orcus (recharges after a short or long rest). *Melee Weapon Attack:* +5 to hit, reach 5 ft., one target. Hit: 11 (2d8 + 2) necrotic damage, and the target's Strength score is reduced by 1d6. The target dies if this reduces its Strength to 0. Otherwise, the reduction lasts until the target finishes a short or long rest.

If a non-evil humanoid dies from this attack, a shadow rises from the corpse in 24 hours under the priest's control, unless the humanoid is restored to life or its body is destroyed. The priest can have no more than four shadows under its control at one time.

Slime Initiate

Medium humanoid (any), any evil alignment

Armor Class 16 (natural armor)
Hit Points 49 (9d8 + 9)
Speed 40 ft.

STR	DEX	CON	INT	WIS	CHA
10 (+0)	16 (+3)	13 (+1)	11 (+0)	16 (+3)	10 (+0)

Saving Throws Dex +5, Wis +5
Skills Acrobatics +5, Stealth +5
Damage Resistance fire
Senses passive Perception 13
Language Common, Abyssal
Challenge 4 (1,100 XP)

Fists of Slime (1/day). The slime initiate wreaths its fists in flame. It deals an additional 7 (2d6) acid damage when it hits with its Unarmed Strikes for 1 minute.

Slow Fall. The slime initiate reduces any falling damage by 30. If it does not take damage from a fall, it does not fall prone.

Actions

Multiattack. The slime initiate makes two Unarmed Strikes. It can use its Flurry of Blows ability in place of one of the Unarmed Strikes.

Unarmed Strike. *Melee Weapon Attack:* +5 to hit, reach 5 ft., one target. *Hit:* 6 (1d6 + 3) bludgeoning damage.

Flurry of Blows (3/day). *Melee Weapon Attack:* +5 to hit, reach 5 ft., one target. *Hit:* 13 (3d6 + 3) bludgeoning damage, and the target suffers one of the following effects of the slime initiate's choice:
• The target must succeed on a DC 14 Dexterity saving throw or be knocked prone.
• The target must make a DC 14 Strength saving throw or be pushed up to 15 feet away from it.
• The target can't take reactions until the end of its next turn.

Litany of Chaos (1/day). The slime initiate chants maniacally, focusing the power of chaos on its enemies. Up to three creatures of the slime initiate's choice that it can see within 50 feet must succeed on a DC 14 Wisdom saving throw or be stunned until the end of the slime mendicant's next turn.

Reactions

Dissolve Missiles. If it has one hand free, the slime initiate can use its reaction in response to being hit with a ranged weapon attack. It reduces the damage by 11 (1d10 + 6). If it reduces the damage to 0, it can completely dissolve the missile if it is small enough for it to hold with one hand.

Slime Mendicant

Medium humanoid (any), any evil alignment

Armor Class 18 (natural armor)
Hit Points 66 (12d8 + 12)
Speed 40 ft.

STR	DEX	CON	INT	WIS	CHA
10 (+0)	18 (+4)	13 (+1)	11 (+0)	18 (+4)	12 (+1)

Saving Throws Dex +7, Wis +7
Skills Acrobatics +7, Stealth +7
Damage Resistance acid
Senses passive Perception 14
Language Common, Abyssal
Challenge 6 (2,300 XP)

Fists of Slime (2/day). The slime mendicant wreaths its fists in slime. It deals an additional 7 (2d6) acid damage when it hits with its Unarmed Strikes for 1 minute.

Slow Fall. The slime mendicant reduces any falling damage by 30. If it does not take damage from a fall, it does not fall prone.

Actions

Multiattack. The slime mendicant makes three Unarmed Strikes. It can use its Flurry of Blows ability in place of one of the Unarmed Strikes.

Unarmed Strike. *Melee Weapon Attack:* +7 to hit, reach 5 ft., one target. *Hit:* 7 (1d6 + 4) bludgeoning damage.

Flurry of Blows (3/day). *Melee Weapon Attack:* +7 to hit, reach 5 ft., one target. *Hit:* 14 (3d6 + 4) bludgeoning damage, and the target suffers one of the following effects of the slime mendicant's choice:
• The target must succeed on a DC 15 Dexterity saving throw or be knocked prone.
• The target must make a DC 15 Strength saving throw or be pushed up to 15 feet away from it.
• The target can't take reactions until the end of its next turn.

Litany of Chaos (2/day). The slime mendicant chants maniacally, focusing the power of chaos on its enemies. Up to three creatures of the slime mendicant's choice that it can see within 50 feet must succeed on a DC 15 Wisdom saving throw or be stunned until the end of the slime mendicant's next turn.

Reactions

Dissolve Missiles. If it has one hand free, the slime mendicant can use its reaction in response to being hit with a ranged weapon attack. It reduces the damage by 11 (1d10 + 6). If it reduces the damage to 0, it can completely dissolve the missile if it is small enough for it to hold with one hand.

STUN JELLY

Large ooze, unaligned

Armor Class 9
Hit Points 57 (6d10 + 24)
Speed 20 ft., climb 20 ft.

STR	DEX	CON	INT	WIS	CHA
14 (+2)	9 (−1)	18 (+4)	1 (−5)	6 (−2)	1 (−5)

Damage Resistances piercing
Damage Immunities acid, cold, lightning, poison
Condition Immunities blinded, charmed, deafened, exhaustion, frightened, poisoned, prone
Senses blindsight 60 ft. (blind beyond this radius), passive Perception 8
Languages —
Challenge 3 (700 XP)

Amorphous. The stunjelly can move through a space as narrow as 1 inch wide without squeezing.

Corrosive Form. A creature that touches the stunjelly or hits it with a melee attack while within 5 feet of it takes 7 (2d6) acid damage. Any nonmagical weapon made of wood or other organic material that hits the stunjelly partly dissolves. After hitting the stunjelly, the weapon takes a permanent and cumulative −1 to damage rolls. If its penalty drops to −5, the weapon is destroyed. Nonmagical ammunition made of wood (or other organic material) that hits the stunjelly is destroyed after dealing damage.

Engulfing. When the stunjelly hits a creature with a Slam attack, it may make one Engulf attack against that creature as a bonus action.

Spider Climb. The stunjelly can climb difficult surfaces, including upside down and ceilings, without needing to make an ability check.

ACTIONS

Slam. *Melee Weapon Attack:* +4 to hit, reach 5 ft., one target. *Hit:* 5 (1d6 + 2) bludgeoning damage plus 7 (2d6) acid damage. If the target is a creature, it must make a DC 14 Constitution saving throw. On a failed save, the creature is paralyzed for 1 minute. The creature may repeat this saving throw at the end of each of its turns, ending the paralysis on itself on a success.

If the creature is wearing armor made of leather or other organic material when hit by the stunjelly, that armor is partly dissolved and takes a permanent and cumulative −1 to the AC it offers. The armor is destroyed if the penalty reduces its AC to 10.

Engulf. The stunjelly attempts to engulf one creature of size Large or smaller within 5 feet of it. The creature must make a DC 15 Dexterity saving throw. On a failed save, the stunjelly enters the creature's space, and the creature takes 7 (2d6) acid damage and is engulfed. The engulfed creature can't breathe, is restrained, and must succeed on a DC 14 Constitution saving throw or be paralyzed for 1 minute. The creature may repeat this Constitution saving throw at the end of each of its turns, ending the paralysis on itself on a success.

At the start of each of the stunjelly's turns, the engulfed creature takes 14 (4d6) acid damage, and any equipment it is carrying made of leather or other organic material is partly dissolved (see Slam above). When the stunjelly moves, the engulfed creature moves with it. An engulfed creature can try to escape by taking an action to make a DC 14 Strength check. On a success, the creature escapes and enters a space of its choice within 5 feet of the stunjelly.

The stunjelly may only engulf 1 Large, 2 Medium, or 4 Small or smaller creatures at one time.

VAMPIRIC OOZE

Large ooze, unaligned

Armor Class 9
Hit Points 95 (10d10 + 40)
Speed 20 ft., climb 20 ft.

STR	DEX	CON	INT	WIS	CHA
16 (+3)	9 (−1)	18 (+4)	1 (−5)	6 (−2)	1 (−5)

Damage Immunities acid, cold, lightning, necrotic, poison, slashing
Condition Immunities blinded, charmed, deafened, exhaustion, frightened, poisoned, prone
Senses blindsight 60 ft. (blind beyond this radius), passive Perception 8
Languages —
Challenge 8 (3,900 XP)

Amorphous. The ooze can move through a space as narrow as 1 inch wide without squeezing.

Spider Climb. The ooze can climb difficult surfaces, including upside down on ceilings, without needing to make an ability check.

ACTIONS

Multiattack. The ooze makes two Pseudopod attacks.

Pseudopod. *Melee Weapon Attack:* +6 to hit, reach 5 ft., one target. *Hit:* 8 (2d4 + 3) bludgeoning damage plus 10 (3d6) necrotic damage. The target's hit point maximum is reduced by an amount equal to the necrotic damage taken, and the ooze regains hit points equal to that amount. If the ooze was at its maximum hit points before this attack, it instead gains temporary hit points equal to the necrotic damage done. The reduction lasts until the target finishes a long rest. The target dies if this effect reduces its hit point maximum to 0. A humanoid slain in this way rises after 1 minute as a zombie spawn under the ooze's control.

REACTIONS

Split. When an ooze that is Medium or larger is subjected to lightning or slashing damage, it splits into two new puddings if it has at least 10 hit points. Each new pudding has hit points equal to half the original pudding's, rounded down. New puddings are one size smaller than the original pudding.

NECROMANCER
Games™